The
House on Curtin Street

By Millie J. Ragosta

THE HOUSE ON CURTIN STREET
WITNESS TO TREASON
KING JOHN'S TREASURE

The
House on Curtin Street

MILLIE J. RAGOSTA

DOUBLEDAY & COMPANY, INC.

GARDEN CITY, NEW YORK

1979

All of the characters in this book are fictitious, and
any resemblance to actual persons, living or dead, is
purely coincidental.

Library of Congress Cataloging in Publication Data

Ragosta, Millie J.
The house on Curtin Street.

1. Bellefonte, Pa.—History—Fiction. I. Title.
PZ4.R143Ho [PS3568.A413]   813'.5'4
ISBN: 0-385-12255-1
Library of Congress Catalog Card Number 78-22539

*For the people of Bellefonte
who made us feel as if we've always lived here and
for all women who dare to attempt great things*

Special thanks to Gladys Murray of the Centre County Library and Historical Society Staff, who assisted me in researching early Bellefonte, Pennsylvania, to Gregory Ramsey of the Centre County Historical Registration Project, who discovered that our house had been built by Miss Minerva Parker and on whose work this fictionalized story is based, and to my son, Joe, who helped me research Miss Parker's work.

CHAPTER 1

I awoke from a fitful doze as the porter called, "Belle-fonte, next stop, Bellefonte."

My throat felt dry and raw and my eyes gritty from the cinders that seemed to penetrate every corner of the rail-road car. They'd settled into the folds of my skirt and I could feel them in my hair and around the neck of my blouse. Even in my ears!

I pulled a small mirror from my pocketbook and propped it against the opposite seat. It afforded me very little vision of myself as I donned my new felt skimmer and tidied my piled up hair. I certainly wasn't looking my best after the long train ride from Philadelphia. My green eyes were red-rimmed and my face looked smudgy and pale. I rubbed futilely at the dirt that seemed to have settled into every pore. I certainly would be grateful for a shampoo and bath!

Still, not even the ponderously slowing train with its clangorous machinery and omnipresent soot could dampen my elation. I, Minerva Stewart, was to design my first house here in this little central Pennsylvania community.

I had received my degree more than a year before and had tried without success to secure a position in some firm of architects. I'd submitted my portfolio again and again, meeting with every reaction from raised eyebrows

to the bald statement that I should go home to the
kitchen where I belonged. One exceptionally obnoxious
interviewer had suggested that I might like to try my
hand designing a "dwelling" for the Saint Bernard puppy
he'd recently purchased for his children. I had stalked
from his office indignantly and later regretted that first
burst of anger I'd allowed myself during all my rejection
and struggle. Even in school there had been opposition to
a woman aspiring to a career in architecture, but I had
thought then that if I worked hard, learned my profession
well and created fine designs, the public would judge me
on my merits as an architect and not upon my sex. How
wrong I had been.

My bitterness was especially potent because designs I'd
submitted to various contests prudently listing myself as
M. J. Stewart had received honorable mentions, and in
one case, first place. Why, when my work did well in
competition where my sex was not known, was I having
so much trouble establishing myself? I was thankful for
my parents' small bequest that had enabled me to live,
however frugally, since finishing school.

I was not one to accept defeat easily, yet as the months
moved along and my small means diminished, I realized I
would soon be forced to find another manner of supporting myself. I knew that I was qualified to be a teacher
and would very likely be accepted if no *man* wanted a
certain post. I liked children, too, and supposed I'd find
great rewards in such a profession. But my heart ached at
the thought of being forced to give up the one thing I'd
longed to do ever since my father had presented me with
a set of building blocks at the age of three. If I had not
been good enough or lacking in talent, I would have accepted it. But to seem to be barred from my heart's desire

simply because I was a woman was almost more than I could bear.

Then, a month before, I had received a letter that had lifted my hopes to heaven again.

"Dear M. J. Stewart," it had begun. "Recently I saw a sample of your designs in an exhibit at the Art Club. I can't tell you too strongly how impressed I was with their ingenuity and originality.

"My wife and I are presently living in Philadelphia but will leave next week to take up residence at her father's home in Bellefonte, Pa., where I have recently accepted a position as manager of the Nittany Coal Company. We, naturally, will be wanting a home in that community and have decided to build one, no dwelling that quite suits our needs being available for purchase at this time. I have taken my wife to see your work, and she agrees with me that we would be delighted to have you design a house for us.

"I realize you are probably inundated with offers in the Philadelphia area and may not want to journey into the hinterlands to undertake a commission. But at any rate, may we call upon you and discuss the possibility of your designing our home?"

The letter was signed, "William J. Tyndall."

I'd written to Mr. Tyndall promptly and set a time when I could meet with him and his wife. I arranged the meeting for lunch at a downtown restaurant for I didn't want them to come to my shabby flat and realize the irony of his letter mentioning my supposed plethora of commissions.

I dressed carefully and simply for the meeting, telling myself to stay calm and not let my foolish heart set itself upon securing the contract. No doubt, when the Tyndalls saw that I was a woman, they'd register immediate embarrassment and find some expedient way to extricate themselves from their offer. I had spent a precious dollar and thirty-nine cents to buy a new hat and collar, inexpensive for 1890, and told myself sternly that if nothing came of this encounter, I would apply to the Board of Education for certification as a school teacher. I would even keep my head modestly bowed and tell them in a hushed and frightened voice that I was all alone in the world, and when my father and mother's legacy was gone would have no means of support. The gentleman in charge would then, no doubt, think I was a brave, gallant little soul who surely ought to be helped until some man came along to offer me honorable marriage. I grimaced as I thought I should be grateful men were willing to trust the welfare of their children's primary education to women. There was little else we were considered fit for. Certainly not for designing the houses we were expected to preside over, cook in and keep clean. Why should it be unwomanly for a girl to design a house but not to break her back cleaning it? Why was it that any woman who felt such an overwhelming desire to excel at work considered proper only for men should be considered a freak, lucky to avoid being labeled a wallflower left drooping on the paternal vine until she slipped apologetically into old age, the pitied and patronized old maid of the town?

I straightened my new collar determinedly and surveyed myself in my cracked mirror. I was a reasonably attractive girl, my dark brown hair being my best feature. My eyes were deep green with thick lashes the same shade as my hair. My nose was a bit short for my face and my mouth too wide for most tastes, I was sure, but I had had two marriage offers. I thought wryly that I tended to judge myself by the very standards I despised—my desirability as a marriage partner. My trouble was that I was incurably romantic. I, like every other girl I knew, wanted to be swept off my feet by a strong and virile man. I wanted to be loved. To be thought a fine, yes, even an incomparable woman. To be considered attractive. A woman to be loved and wooed and won.

I didn't want much, I said with a grimace at my own reflection in the mirror. Only the moon. So far I hadn't met a man who didn't consider my interest in architecture an aberration. Perhaps it would be all to the good, therefore, if Mr. Tyndall did beat a hasty retreat upon discovering that I was a woman. Perhaps if I failed as an architect even without a fair chance, I'd be willing to settle into a more conventional role for a woman.

But even as I told myself so, I knew it *wasn't* so. I would never be happy until I could build the beautiful homes that lived in my imagination. I knew that I had something to offer the world. Especially the women's world. For I had watched my own mother struggle with housework in great monstrous houses with eighteen-foot ceilings and dark kitchens. I knew how hard her lot had been. I envisioned houses bright with fewer, larger windows, manageable ceiling heights, laundry rooms with proper facilities and access to the outside clothesline, kitchens with adequate work surfaces and cupboards so a small woman wouldn't have to climb upon a stool to reach the shelves. I envisioned houses men would never dream of building, but which women would bless me for. I wanted with all my heart and soul to be able to design them.

And I knew, moreover, that I'd never be happy with

any man who'd deny me the right to follow my heart's desire.

I arrived at the restaurant a bit early so I could identify myself to the head waiter and thus spare Mr. Tyndall embarrassment of searching in vain for a man named M. J. Stewart. I allowed him to show me to a small table near the front of the dining room and left to him the responsibility of asking arrivals if they were William J. Tyndall and wife.

In a very short while, the waiter ushered a man and a woman toward my table. The woman was slender and lovely with an aristocratic carriage and an elegant black bombazine suit that became her well. Her smile as she glanced at her husband was very warm and spoke of real friendship between the two. Her eyes were black and sparkling, her hair auburn and simply dressed. The bones of her face were prominent and graceful and the flash of white teeth her smile afforded, charming. Her husband was only an inch or two taller than she but broad-shouldered and well made. His hair was thick and curly but beginning to recede a bit at the forehead. Deep gray eyes met mine, and I tried to read surprise in them as he saw that I was a woman. I began to rise nervously, realizing that I was meeting them in a business capacity. Under ordinary social circumstances, of course, I would remain seated. Suddenly panicky, I couldn't decide whether to continue rising, to remain seated in a ladylike way, to extend my hand, to speak to them or allow him to introduce them to me first.

He must have seen my uneasiness for he smiled and made a motion that I should stay seated.

Mrs. Tyndall smiled warmly at me. "I told you, Bill, it

is a woman," she said softly. "I knew it the minute I saw those designs."

He laughed and held his wife's chair, motioning the waiter away with an easy grace. "So that explains the initials. My wife insisted that you'd long since learned not to use your Christian name. I see she is right."

"I am sorry, Mr. Tyndall," I found myself babbling uncertainly. "Of course, if you object, you need feel no obligation . . ."

His wife frowned suddenly and reached out to tap my hand as it lay on the table. The action was slight and almost playful, and she laughed with mild exasperation to lessen even that effect. "I beg you, Miss Stewart, don't dare ever apologize," she commanded. "It *is Miss* Stewart, isn't it?"

"Yes. I'm not married."

"Please don't mind that I'm so brusque," she continued, "but a woman who has your talent for design should not apologize for anything, much less being a woman."

"It's so kind of you to say that," I said, warming to her encouragement, "but the minute anyone finds out I'm a female, they seem shocked and inclined to withdraw from any business connection with me."

Mr. Tyndall nodded and threw his wife a wry smile. "I am just beginning to realize the truth of that, Miss Stewart. My wife dins it into my head at every opportunity. I must confess, since she's been calling my attention to it, I have seen evidence of such circumstances all around me. If I were a woman, fortunate to be blessed with talent and ability in this ridiculous world of ours, I am sure I'd be so frustrated at every turn I would scarcely be able to function."

"Then, you honestly don't *mind* that I allowed you to believe I was a man?" I said, heartened.

"You didn't really *allow* us to believe that," he replied judicially. "You simply used your initials as many men do. I would say your deception was minimal and quite justified." He leaned back easily in his chair and made a gesture of summons to the waiter who was waiting discreetly for us to be ready to order. "Indeed, had I been in your place, I don't doubt I'd have been tempted to hire a male actor to keep this appointment."

I laughed. "I never thought of that," I said. "I wonder if it would have worked."

We ordered then and the conversation about the commission necessarily stopped. After the waiter retired, Mrs. Tyndall spoke.

"I am so happy Bill happened to see your designs, Miss Stewart. They are so exactly what I've been wanting. Every architect we've talked to seems intent upon creating bigger and bigger monstrosities to excite the envy of his colleagues, whereas we want a *family* house. Large enough to allow us all plenty of privacy when we need it, but not resembling Buckingham Palace."

"Oh, I'm so glad. That's exactly what I've tried to accomplish with the designs I've done. Though, unfortunately, I've never been able to see a finished product yet." I sipped my water quickly, wishing I'd not admitted that.

Mr. Tyndall laughed. "Darling," he said to his wife, "I think you really ought to take Miss Stewart to one of your suffragette meetings. She could do with a bit of confidence in herself."

I blushed deeply. Suddenly I felt very young and foolish. But I knew they were laughing with me and not at me, and so I was not intimidated. "I have had few opportunities to gain any confidence in myself," I admitted and found myself telling them the story of my offer to build a dog "dwelling." They laughed heartily at the story, then Mrs. Tyndall bridled.

"You see, Bill? Isn't that insupportable?" she said, still half-laughing. "I tell you, it's a poor man who'd insult an architect of her ability with such a preposterous proposition."

"Don't be so hard on him, Alice. You must admit, it isn't every day an architectural firm has a young lady apply for work."

"Exactly so. All the more reason they should admire her pluck at getting herself accredited and bend over backward to give her a chance."

He grinned suddenly, his face looking almost impish as if the argument was an old and enjoyable one between them. "Ah, darling, you are crusading for equal rights for women, then promptly show that you want *special* rights by thinking the world should 'bend over backward' for your sex."

She laughed and touched his hand lightly. "You're right, Bill. That's exactly what I said. I suppose I'm used to expecting men's gallantry as a right, yet want equality, too. It is a problem, isn't it?"

"You must learn to be more reasonable and moderate if you would really help women like Miss Stewart," he said. Then, turning to me, "But we have in mind a far more practical means of helping you, Miss Stewart. We've already agreed we like your designs and want you to be our architect. But we'd like you to see the land we've bought for our home before you go ahead. Would you be able to spend some time in Bellefonte?"

I could hardly contain my excitement. "Oh, yes, sir. Any time you want me there. I am at your disposal."

Mrs. Tyndall shook her head in feigned disapproval. "You should tell him you'll check your calendar, my dear," she said, and we all laughed.

As the waiter brought the entree, we began discussing the Tyndalls' needs. And by the time lunch was finished, they had insisted that I follow them to Bellefonte. They were to leave Philadelphia by the end of the week; I, by the end of the month.

I thought that the Tyndalls themselves would be at the station to meet me when I arrived in Bellefonte, but there was no one on the platform except an elderly gentleman with thick, silvery hair and inquisitive dark eyes. He smiled uncertainly at me and came forward to assist me as I descended from the train.

"Are you Minerva Stewart, miss?" he asked.

"Yes, I am," I replied, waiting for him to continue.

He bowed his head in a quaint, courtly gesture, then took my reticule from my hand. "I am Jonathon Bosworth, Alice Tyndall's father," he explained. "Alice had intended to meet you but her child, my granddaughter, Annette, had a piano recital this morning and her mother was reluctant to miss it when your wire came. Bill had to go to the mine, and so I volunteered to meet your train. I hope you're not disappointed."

"Of course not. I'm delighted to meet you, sir," I said, extending my hand. "I'm sorry you had to miss your granddaughter's recital, though."

He chuckled wickedly. "I'm not. But don't tell Annette. She's developed very little skill at this point."

"How old is she?"

"Seven. And the apple of my eye in spite of her music."

He led the way to a light buggy to which a fine chestnut carriage horse was hitched. The conveyance sat across the street from the station in front of a four-story hotel with BUSH HOUSE in large letters across the brick facade. The hotel was surprisingly spacious for such a town—the Tyndalls had told me the population was only a few thousand—and loomed high above a shallow, rapidly flowing stream almost like a mill building. Spanning the stream was a small bridge perhaps thirty feet above the water. As we crossed to the buggy, my host pointed out the county courthouse at the top of the ascending street on the other side of the bridge. It sat in the morning sunlight, Corinthian pillars gleaming, like the little town's proud guardian. On either side of the street leading to the courthouse were brick and stone dwellings, most with businesses on the ground floors that opened right onto the sidewalk.

Mr. Bosworth handed me into the buggy and patted the horse's flank absently. "If you'll excuse me for one moment, Miss Stewart, I've got a small errand in the Bush House. I'll be with you directly."

"Of course. It will be pleasant to sit here admiring your lovely little town," I said.

"If you look carefully, you'll see my son, Jonathon, Jr.'s office there on the right slightly below the courthouse," he said. "He is recently graduated from Temple University Medical School and has set up practice here."

"How nice for you," I observed.

He made his way back into the Bush House, and I settled back to survey the town as I waited. The October afternoon was sunny and bright with scraps of foliage remaining on the trees, but it was nearly Halloween and the air was bitingly cold here in the mountains. I reached for an old buffalo robe in the back of the carriage beside my baggage and spread it over my lap. I was glad I'd worn my winter coat and turned its collar up to protect my face from the icy wind that blew along the creek basin.

Suddenly something crashed to the brick-paved road directly in front of the horse's nose. The report as it hit was explosive, and the horse, even more startled than I, reared high into the air, screaming in fright, then came down hard and dashed toward the bridge.

I had nearly been thrown out by the initial jolt and now saw that I was almost certain to be when the buggy inevitably hit the bridge railing. The water, far below was too shallow to allow me the safety of a mere dunking if I should hit in that direction. I could see all this in a split second, and though I didn't quite assimilate it, I found the presence of mind to lunge to the right onto the roadway and away from the railing.

I felt a jarring pain as my feet hit the hard paving, then a jolting at the knees as they took the impact. I fell, rolling onto my hip and shoulder and felt a searing as my palms, in a vain effort to absorb the fall, scraped along the brick. My head struck the sidewalk but, fortunately, with far less impact than it would have had I not taken the worst of the fall with hip and shoulder. I hurt all over and my heart was thumping with fright, but I realized I was not too badly hurt. I tried to scramble to my feet but was still too shaky for that.

The horse had demolished the buggy in her headlong flight up the hill. The remains of it dragged behind her, scattering debris and causing her more terror than ever. I saw people running to escape her path and a few men trying to grab at her harness. Then, perhaps attracted by the noise the horse had made before she bolted, people began running out from the hotel.

I realized suddenly that my skirts were clear up about my thighs exposing stockings and drawers and petticoats. I fumbled at them shakily and managed to get myself a bit more circumspect before anyone reached my side.

"Are you hurt, miss?" a masculine voice above my head asked, and I turned to look into a pair of deep blue eyes beneath a felt hat. The man who was standing looking down at me had come, it seemed, from the railroad station across the way. His eyes flickered along my inert form quickly as he knelt to my aid. He was dressed in riding boots and jacket and had a lean, sunbrowned face that seemed anxious now about my welfare.

"I'm quite all right," I replied, struggling to a sitting position. "I'll be able to get up in a moment."

"Lucky you weren't killed," he said. "No doubt you would have been if you hadn't jumped."

"I don't know what happened. Something hit the road in front of the horse, I think . . ."

Mr. Bosworth, his face white and strained, pushed the young man away and knelt at my side. "Jenny, Jenny, are you hurt?" he cried distractedly.

I stared at him in astonishment. "I'm fine, Mr. Bosworth. And my name is Minerva, not Jenny."

But he seemed not to hear me. "Get a doctor. Oh, someone, go get my son, Jon. Tell him his mother's been hurt."

The young man who had reached me first put a reassuring arm about Mr. Bosworth's shoulders. "Jon will be here in a moment, sir." He made a motion to one of the men from the hotel, who promptly ran up the street to-

ward the office Mr. Bosworth had pointed out to me as his
son's.

"I'm quite all right. I am Minerva Stewart, Mr. Bosworth," I said, trying to still his rising agitation. "Please,
please calm yourself."

He stared at me wildly, and partly to reassure him,
partly because I was deeply embarrassed by the attention, I struggled to my feet, swaying a little. The young
man in riding boots hastened to steady me, then led me to
a bench sitting in front of the hotel.

"He's confused, young lady," he whispered. "His wife
disappeared last spring, and he hasn't gotten over his
grief. Though to my knowledge, this is the first he's mis-
taken someone else for her. Usually, he thinks she's just
gone out for a while and will be back." He helped me
lower myself to the bench, and I looked at the old gentleman with understanding.

"How terrible," I murmured. "Oh, do see to him. I'm
perfectly all right."

Just then the doctor, a younger version of Mr. Bosworth, whose blond hair was nearly as light as his father's snow-white mane, came dashing down the hill in
his waistcoat, his black bag clutched firmly in his hand.

"They've caught your horse, Father," he said to Mr.
Bosworth. "What on earth happened? Are you all
right?"

The young man who'd first helped me answered for Mr.
Bosworth. "He's all right, Jon, it was this young lady who
was in the buggy at the time."

The newcomer turned his attention to me. I waved my
hand deprecatingly. "I am really quite all right. My
heavy coat protected me in the fall, and I'm no more than
thoroughly shaken. It's your father who is really upset."

The few onlookers, seeing that I was unhurt, moved away to where the quivering mare, recaptured now by a burly man in farmer's overalls, was being unharnessed from the wreckage that had been the buggy. The young man in riding boots, taking advantage of the general attention being turned away from myself and Mr. Bosworth, went and gently guided the old man to sit beside me on the bench. "He's not himself, Jon," he said with a meaningful glance at the doctor.

Jon nodded in quick comprehension and put a steadying hand on his father's arm. "Father, it's all right," he said gently. "The young lady, Miss Stewart?"—this with a quick glance at me for confirmation—"is quite all right. You mustn't be upset."

"Your mother had a terrible fall from the carriage, son," the old gentleman said in a quavery voice. "But I believe she's unhurt."

"It's Miss Stewart, Father. Not Mother. Miss Stewart." The young doctor seemed to be holding distress under firm control as he spoke to his father. I studied his profile as he bent over him. His skin was very fair and he had light gray eyes. He was tall and powerfully built as was his father. I didn't think he looked much like Mrs. Tyndall, his sister.

Mr. Bosworth calmed down noticeably under his son's hands. He looked at me searchingly. "I seem to have become confused. I hope I haven't made a complete fool of myself, Miss Stewart. Do forgive me," he said at last.

I laid a hand on his sleeve. "It's nothing, sir. It was enough to confuse anyone. It happened so fast."

"What *did* happen?" Jon asked. "I've never known Duchess to bolt like that."

"I don't know exactly," I said, looking toward the spot

on the roadway where the carriage had been. "Something seemed almost to explode right under the horse's hooves."

My "rescuer," apparently a friend of the family, walked over to examine the area. He knelt down and presently came back with something in his hand. He extended it toward Jon. It was a bit of brick freshly splintered.

"What on earth would do that?" Jon said wonderingly. "It seems freshly broken."

The young man cleared his throat and shook his head. "The only thing I can think of is a bullet," he said. "A hunter must have gotten off a wild shot, perhaps from the ridge above town."

"I will report it to the sheriff's office immediately," said Mr. Bosworth indignantly. "How nearly tragic that careless shot was. Why, Miss Stewart is lucky to be alive. And it's really remarkable Duchess wasn't harmed."

"You're right, Father. Thank heaven they were both unhurt. Your buggy is a shambles."

The old man shook his head worriedly. I could see that he was still quite shaken by the incident. He reached out to touch me as if to reassure himself that I was all right. "I haven't even introduced you to my son or to Richard, here, who came to our aid so kindly. Miss Minerva Stewart, the architect Bill and Alice have engaged, allow me to present my son, Dr. Jonathon Bosworth, and Mr. Richard Langley, Bill's assistant. Indeed, Bill assures me that Richard is the most capable mining engineer he's ever had the pleasure of working with."

I acknowledged the introduction and thanked both men for their concern. A passerby, having retrieved my baggage and the lap robe that had been thrown clear of the buggy, brought them forward.

"You'll not be driving the young lady anywhere in *that*

rig, Mr. Bosworth," he said matter-of-factly. "I'd be honored if you'd let me drive you home."

My host graciously accepted the offer, then, frowning, turned to me. "That is, if you feel able to get into the carriage, Miss Stewart," he added solicitously. "Jon should look you over first."

"Oh, I'm really quite all right," I said, standing up to demonstrate that I could with ease. "A good hot bath will be all I'll need to set me right."

Dr. Jon smiled and nodded in agreement. "The hotter the better. I'd say the most ill effects you're likely to have will be a great many aches and pains tomorrow. The bath should help. Then go to bed. I'm sure you're exhausted from your trip. I'll examine you when I get home at noon."

"I'm sure there's no need to waste your skill, Doctor, though I do thank you."

"Jon, please report the incident to the sheriff," Mr. Bosworth added as he handed me into the rig our benefactor had brought around. "He really must be more stern with these careless people who call themselves sportsmen."

"I will, Father. I'll see you at lunch, Miss Stewart."

"And I'll see you both at dinner tonight," said Richard Langley with a charming smile. "Now that I have met you, Miss Stewart, I'm doubly happy that Mr. Tyndall invited me to help welcome you to Bellefonte."

I thanked them both again and leaned back between Mr. Bosworth and our driver, introduced by Mr. Bosworth as P. Gray Meek, editor of the local newspaper. The horse, Duchess, had been hitched to the rear of the rig and followed docilely enough now. Indeed, she seemed to have recovered herself more rapidly than I, for I found that I was still shaking. It was lucky I was not a superstitious person, I thought, or I'd consider the incident a most unpropitious welcome to Bellefonte.

The Bosworth home was a large white frame house with a two-story widow's walk, all enclosed with glass windows. It was on the corner of a finished street, Spring, and a wagon track marked Curtin, right at the edge of town. Beyond it the woods and hills stretched off to a low mountain range, so although the house was part of the borough, it enjoyed a rural isolation.

Mr. Bosworth waved his hand toward the north. "The land my son-in-law bought for his house is up that way. A hundred acres· or better. I really don't know why he would want it, it's so rough. Especially when this house has enough room and to·spare for all of us."

Mr. Meek chuckled. "Young people want a house of their own, Jonathon. It was fine for Bill and Alice and the child to stay with you for holidays and vacations while he was still in Philadelphia, but now that he's been sent to Bellefonte permanently, I can understand their desire to have a place of their own. Face it, my friend, you just don't want them to move out of your house."

My host smiled abashedly. "You're right. I'll miss Annette always being at my heels."

"They'll be only a short walk away. You'll see them often."

The editor held his horse steady while he descended from the rig, and Mr. Bosworth unhitched Duchess from the rear. Then with a friendly nod in answer to our thanks, he drove back toward town.

An elderly black man opened the double front door and came toward us, smiling. But when he saw the absence of Mr. Bosworth's buggy and the horse being led by a bit of the hitching apparatus, he hurried forward anxiously. "Where's the rig, Mr. Bosworth? Is somethin' wrong?"

"Everything's all right now, George. Don't worry," my host said. "A careless hunter shot too close to the horse and caused her to bolt. The carriage is wrecked beyond repair, I'm afraid. After you see to Duchess, I'd appreciate your going down to the Bush House and arranging to have it hauled away."

"Lands, sir, you sure you all right?" the old man asked, and Mr. Bosworth had some trouble reassuring him. Then, turning to me, he laughed and shook his head.

"Miss Stewart, this is George. He's been here with us for twenty-eight years now."

The old negro smiled proudly and ran a hand along Duchess' flank. "Yes, miss, I comed here because a man down in Lancaster tol' me Mr. Bosworth in Bellefonte has got a secrut room to hide slaves in so they can rest on the way to Canada."

"Really?" I said excitedly. "This house was a stop on the Underground Railroad?"

He nodded delightedly and rubbed his grizzled head. "Yes, miss. They say you's the ark'tec' lady who's gonna figger how to build a house for Miss Alice and Mr. Bill. I thought you'd like to know about the room."

My host was smiling indulgently at the old man. "You can show it to her tomorrow when she's rested, George."

"Oh, I'd like that," I said. "But how was it that you didn't go on to Canada, George? I thought it was dangerous for escaped slaves to stay in the United States at that time."

"He refused to go," Mr. Bosworth growled amiably. "When it was time for him to move on, the old rascal just wouldn't go. It was a good thing for me President Lincoln signed the Emancipation Proclamation that September, or I'd have been in trouble for shielding him. And now I suppose he'll never go," Mr. Bosworth growled, but his eyes smiled fondly on the old negro. "Well, the least you can do is to take care of that horse. No, on second thought, I'll do that, you show Miss Stewart to her room. She's to go right to bed after she's had a bath. But you see she has a nice tray of lunch in her room and that no one disturbs her, George, you hear?"

"Yes sir, Mr. Bosworth," George said amiably, taking my reticule which I'd set at my feet. "You come along, Miss Stewart. You do look fit to drop."

He led me through the double doors into a tiny foyer with a similar set of double doors that stood invitingly open to a spacious center hall. Wide stairs ascended in a straight line at the rear of the hall. There were more double doors opening off each side of the hall at the foot of the stairs and other single doors farther down. As George led me toward the stairs, I caught glimpses of parlors, the one on the left perhaps thirty by fifteen feet, the one on the right, fifteen by fifteen. Both were graced with black-marble mantels and tall, twelve-paned windows. Fires were burning evenly from gas logs in the fireplaces.

The bedroom he showed me to on the second floor was also heated with a gas log in a fireplace. It was a sunny, pleasant room in the front of the house near the bathroom, and I noted gratefully the big four-poster bed spread with a beautifully woven coverlet. George bustled about, drawing blinds and adjusting the gas. He opened a drawer and pulled out a great pile of snowy towels and spread them on a maple rack near the fireplace.

"You just take all the time you want, miss," he said kindly. "And when you're ready to eat, you just ring that bell there on the mantel. I'll be listenin' and will bring you a good, hot lunch."

"That sounds just wonderful, George. I'll be grateful," I said, removing my somewhat battered hat. "You've all been so kind."

"That's all right, miss. Mr. Bosworth and me, we're happy to do anything to make Miss Alice and Mr. Bill happy. Even if they're gonna move out o' this house."

"Mr. Bosworth seems to love them very much," I said politely.

"He sure does. Them and Mr. Jon and Miss Clarice, too."

"Oh? I've met Mr. Jon, but not Miss Clarice. Is she his wife?" I said, remembering that he still called Mrs. Tyndall *Miss* Alice, too.

"Oh, no, miss, she's his sister. Mr. Jon ain't married. Miss Clarice, she at the piano recital with Miss Alice and Miss Annette. You'll meet her at dinner."

I nodded and began to unpack. But George didn't yet withdraw. He seemed to want to say something to me, and I turned and smiled encouragingly at him.

"Miss, I just want to say, old Mr. Bosworth, he ain't been hisself since his missus disappeared. You mustn't mind if he do seem a bit confused at times."

"I understand, George," I said gently. "He did have a bit of a lapse at the Bush House when the horse bolted, but Mr. Langley was there and he explained. I'm so sorry. It must be a terrible strain for him to have something like that happen."

He nodded sadly. "No one knows where she went. She was a lady who liked to roam 'bout the hills and woods. She knew more 'bout herbs and trees and flowers than a witch woman in the quarters on my old plantation. We never worried none about her when she went into the woods because she always knowed how to take care of herself.

"But one day last spring, she just never come back. We didn't know what happened. The sheriff, he got most of the men in the county out lookin' for her, but they never found no trace."

I thought of the careless gunshot that had panicked Duchess and wondered silently if something similar had happened to Mrs. Bosworth. Perhaps some negligent hunter had shot her, then, frightened, had concealed her body. As if he'd been reading my mind, George sighed.

"We looked for a sign of a grave, but never found none."

"The sheriff had no idea what could have become of her?" I asked gently.

"Well, him and some of the old-timers around here think she might have wandered off somewhere to the west and gotten lost," he said, shaking his head. "There's miles and miles o' nothin' but mountains and woods out there. If she did do that and starved to death, the wild cats would likely have removed any trace o' her. Or they just might never have come across her. Like I say, it's a big country out there."

I shivered and felt a wave of deep sympathy for the elderly woman stumbling confused through the wilderness. How frightened she must have been.

"It must be terrible for Mr. Bosworth and the family not to know what happened," I said sympathetically.

"Sure is. They all suffer. But the chillun, they young and they cheerful folk. They say their mother wouldn't like them to fret, and she'd rather have died out in them woods she loved so much than sittin' in a parlor drinkin' tea till she old and sick. But the old man . . ." He shook his head sadly. "Sometimes he seems to realize she's gone and then he looks to be getting over it, but there're times when he say, 'Jenny just stepped out for a minute; she be right back.' That's terrible," he said. "Once he even thought Miss Alice was his wife."

I nodded solemnly, remembering his reaction when he thought I'd been hurt.

"I'm glad you're here, miss," the old man said more cheerfully. "Mr. Bosworth, he put a heap of stock in being a good host. It will do him good having a nice young lady here. He said we'd all have to do our best to show you Bellefonte's best hospitality."

I smiled and picked up two of the warm towels. "You have certainly made a good start, George," I said. "I'm glad you told me about Mrs. Bosworth. And I hope my presence will prove to be a distraction for Mr. Bosworth. Sometimes it takes quite a while for grief to lessen," I added, thinking of my parents' deaths.

He nodded in agreement, and I saw tears in his own eyes as he turned to leave the room.

CHAPTER 2

A gentle tapping at my door awakened me. I sat up drowsily and pulled on my robe which I'd thrown across the foot of the bed before falling asleep. The room was dark, the only illumination from the gas log. I winced as I threw my legs over the edge of the bed and fastened the cord of my dressing gown. Every bone in my body seemed to ache.

"Come in," I called.

The door opened and a little girl stepped in, shutting the door quietly behind her. She was dressed in a dark smock covered with a long white pinafore. A big ribbon at the back of her head held her hair away from her face. Her eyes widened in the semi-darkness and she put out a hand as if to feel her way.

I hurried to light the gas fixtures on the wall at either side of the fireplace.

"You must be Annette Tyndall," I said conversationally as the gas sputtered into flame. "How do you do?"

She dropped me a polite curtsy and smiled a little shyly. "Yes, I'm Annette. Mother sent me to wake you, Miss Stewart. She said to tell you dinner will be in an hour."

"My! I have been a lazy bones," I said, stifling a yawn. "I suppose I was more tired than I realized. Thank you for waking me. I might have slept right through dinner."

She made a little grimace. "You wouldn't have missed much if you had. It's trout tonight."

"Don't you like trout?" I asked with a smile. "I think it's wonderful."

"I suppose you would. Most grown-ups do, I guess. I don't like fish much. But I'm eating in the kitchen with George and Mary, his wife, tonight and Mary said I could have beaten biscuits and the chicken left from Sunday, so it's all right."

"Oh, I'm glad you don't have to eat the trout if you don't like it."

She stalked over to the bed and hitched herself up onto the edge, holding onto the poster to steady herself. Her eyes followed me attentively.

"You really don't look like an old war horse," she said solemnly.

"Oh? Am I supposed to?" I said, trying not to laugh at her slow, studied way of speaking.

She stared at me frankly as if weighing her words. She was a pretty, fragile-looking child with delicate skin and big dark eyes.

"Well," she said, drawing the word out, "I guess I really don't know what a lady architect looks like, but Tony said very likely you'd be a veritable old war horse who couldn't get a man."

I couldn't help laughing at the serious way she'd repeated a remark she obviously was not meant to hear, but I felt a quick rush of anger toward the unknown Tony too. I picked up my brush and began tidying my hair.

"Who is Tony, Annette?" I said casually.

"Oh, he's an architect, too. He comes around to see Aunt Clarice. *She* says she doesn't know why Mother and Dad didn't let Tony design the house."

I began piling up my hair, smoothing it with the brush. It was fly-away from its recent washing and took all my concentration, though I was glad for the diversion because, judging from her reflection in the mirror, this wide-eyed child was staring at me in a most penetrating way.

"Have you had an unhappy love affair?" was her next startling question.

"Why, no, dear. Whatever gave you that idea?" I said in surprise.

"Oh, Mother told Clarice and Tony you were not a war horse but very pretty and young, and Clarice said that p'rhaps you'd had an unhappy love affair and that was why you'd become a lady architect."

"Oh, no, Annette. I *wanted* to be an architect. With all my heart," I said firmly. Let her take *that* back to Clarice and Tony.

She slid off the bed and came to stand beside me, examining my reflection in the dressing table mirror. "You are very pretty," she said shyly. "I'll bet a lot of men would want to marry you."

"Thank you, Annette. You're very sweet," I said, putting the last comb into my hair.

She sighed elaborately, still staring at me. "I wish one of them would," she said. "Then, p'rhaps, you'd not be designing a house for Dad and Mother."

"Aren't you happy about the idea, Annette?" I said, surprised.

"Oh, it'll be nice, I s'pose," she said grudgingly. "But I'd really rather stay here just now."

I remembered what Mr. Bosworth had said to Mr. Meek about his attachment to Annette and hers to him. "Is it because of your grandfather?" I asked quietly.

She shifted uncomfortably. "That, of course. He *needs* me."

"But you'll be only a few minutes' walk away. You can see him anytime you've a mind to. Stop on your way to and from school."

She thrust her lip out stubbornly. "Oh, I expected you'd say that. After all, you want to build the house."

I laughed uncomfortably. She was certainly a disconcerting child. "I'm sorry you feel that way, Annette. Of course I want to build the house. But, you see, I *am* doing that, regardless of how you feel about it, so that isn't the reason I was trying to cheer you up. I really am sorry you feel so badly about leaving your grandfather and think you're making too much of it. He'll be practically next door. And think how nice it will be for you and your parents to extend *your* hospitality to him sometimes."

She seemed to consider that for a moment. Then she fetched another deep sigh. But she followed it with a tremulous smile. "I guess you're right. I'm sorry I said you only cared about building the house."

"That's all right. I know how it feels to have changes in your life. You've already moved away from Philadelphia just recently, and to have to move again makes a person a bit edgy."

She stared down at her hands as they lay on the dressing table and began worriedly fidgeting with a ragged fingernail. "That isn't the only change that's happened to us," she said in a small voice. "The worst one was Grandma getting lost." Her voice quavered and I saw a tear drop onto her little hands. Impulsively, I reached out and put an arm about her, drawing her to my side.

"I know about that. It's very sad. And you're a dear little girl to be so concerned with your grandfather. I'm sure you're the greatest comfort he could possibly have."

She put her face against my shoulder and I could feel that she was struggling to control herself, not wanting to cry. At last she straightened up and dashed at the tears on her cheek.

"Miss Stewart," she said haltingly, "do you think it would be breaking a promise to someone if I had to do something I really couldn't help? Something that someone else made me do?"

I studied the woebegone face intently. Had Mr. Bosworth been urging her to stay with him? Had he made her promise not to leave his home? I felt at a great disadvantage being placed in the position of judge by this mite. I cleared my throat, trying to think how to answer her without seeming to disapprove of her beloved grandfather. "Annette," I said slowly, "sometimes, when people are shattered with sorrow, they make demands on us that they'd never think of doing if they were perfectly themselves."

She looked up in surprise. "You think I'm talking about Grandad," she said. "*He* hasn't asked me to promise anything."

"Who then, honey? Would you like to tell me?"

She twisted the edge of her pinafore. "It was Grandma. Before she got lost that day," she said in a tiny voice. "We'd been up from Philadelphia so that Dad could have an interview with Mr. Roberts about him going to work here. Grandma wanted to go out to dig some sassafras root to make tea. She said it cleansed the blood in the spring.

"But Grandad didn't feel well. And he didn't want Grandma to go. He was always fussing at her because she

liked to roam around the woods and hills. So, when he fell
asleep, she put on her old boots and jacket and got her
basket. She told me please to stay with Grandad and take
care of him. Not to think of leaving him until she came
back."

I stared at her sympathetically. "And you feel you'd be
breaking your promise to your Grandma if you leave him
now?" I asked.

She shook her head up and down. "I know it's silly. I
know she meant to be back in an hour or so. We had to go
back to Philadelphia later that night, and she knew I'd
have to go then. Of course, when she didn't come back,
we didn't go back to Philadelphia for two weeks. And we
took Grandad with us then. Later, I came back here on
the train with him, so I really haven't left him since I
made her the promise." She drew a long, shuddering
breath. "Yet," she amended.

I reached out and took the little hand which was still
twisting in and out of the lace strap of her pinafore. "Oh,
Annette, don't you see that your grandma never knew
she'd not be coming back. She wanted to be sure someone
was with your grandad while he was ill. She didn't mean
to saddle you with being his little guardian for the rest of
his life."

"I know that, Miss Stewart," she said with the air of
explaining to someone who just hasn't grasped the point,
"and he *did* get over the grippe that made him feel bad
then. But he's sick in a different way now." She paused,
staring up at me as if wondering how much it was pru-
dent to say to me.

"I understand about your grandad not having quite
grasped that your grandma is gone, honey," I said quietly.

"He *needs* me," she said simply, but with a trace of anguish.

"Have you talked this over with your parents, Annette?" I asked, thinking she seemed to be struggling with too big a problem for such a little girl.

She shook her head. "No. They've enough problems of their own just now. Part of the reason Dad took this new position was so we could be nearer Grandad and Grandma. I s'pose they'd think I was being silly, too. As you say, I'll just be a minute away from Grandad." She sighed deeply and rested her face on her hand.

"Well, it will be a long time before the house is actually finished, Annette," I said, mentioning the only thing in the way of comfort I could think of, "and no doubt, by then your grandfather will be quite himself again. And will truly understand that your grandmother is gone. Then his grief will gradually lighten."

She stared at the gas log moodily. "I hope so. But it will take a long time for his grief to lighten, Miss Stewart. He and Grandma fought and fussed a lot, but he truly loved her. He misses her more than you can believe."

She straightened up and smiled wistfully at me, moving back toward the door. "I'd best go and let you get dressed," she said as she reached it. "Some guests are expected for dinner, and likely they'll be here soon."

"Thank you for waking me," I said. "Try not to worry any more about your grandfather."

"I'll truly try, but I just can't seem to help it," she said like an aged dame with the sorrows of years upon her.

I had only one rather shabby green-moire dinner dress which seemed hardly suitable for a family evening, so I donned a white lace blouse and a gray tweed skirt. My mother's cameo brooch was ornament enough, I thought as I fastened it at my throat. Then taking a clean handkerchief from my reticule, which I hadn't completely unpacked yet, I left my room and started down the long stairs.

Mrs. Tyndall was awaiting me at the bottom of the stairs. She was dressed in a simple blue dress with a white collar which reassured me considerably about my own choice of clothes. She smiled a warm welcome as I descended the stairs.

"Welcome to Bellefonte," she said. "And in the same breath, forgive me for not meeting you myself. After I learned that Annette was to be included in the piano recital, there was not time to let you know I could not meet that particular train. I hadn't thought she would be; we'd been here such a short time. But her new teacher wanted to make her feel at home."

"Oh, really, it was quite all right, Mrs. Tyndall," I said, taking the slim hand she proffered. "I enjoyed having a chance to get acquainted with your father."

"My brother, Jon, tells me that there was a dreadful mishap and you might have been killed. Something really must be done about the carelessness of some hunters. He said they think it was a stray bullet that stampeded the horse."

"Well, thank goodness I am durable and no harm was done," I said to reassure her. "I am quite all right."

"I understand Father quite amazed you, thinking you were my mother," she said, lowering her voice a bit. "Jon said he'd intended to explain more fully to you that he's still confused over her disappearance last spring, but you were sleeping when he got home, and he didn't want to disturb you since your injuries seemed minor."

"I'm glad he didn't. And, I want to assure you you need not worry about any explanations. The young man, Richard Langley, who, I gather, is your husband's assistant, managed to explain in a general way at the scene of the accident when your father seemed upset. Then, when I got here . . ." I hesitated, thinking perhaps I should not mention George's discussing his employer's condition.

She laughed abruptly. "George told you all about it," she finished for me.

"He only wanted to explain in case I thought Mr. Bosworth confused," I hastened to say.

"It's quite all right, Miss Stewart. George loves my father as much as I do, and he understands him even more. I know anything he said was from concern and kindness."

"Yes. It certainly was. And I am so sorry about the tragedy."

"We've all come to terms with it. It's hard to think of what her last hours must have been like, alone and lost, but likely she died of exposure, not starvation. The nights were still quite cold then. We try not to brood and just thank the Lord for all the good years she had. All of us except Father. He hasn't adjusted. But I'm convinced that in time he will. He's a good man and a strong one."

She took my arm and guided me toward the large parlor. "Everyone has arrived. I hope you don't object to making an entrance," she said. "Actually, I waited to have Annette wake you until I was certain you'd be the last to gather. I think it will be easier for you to meet all our guests at one time."

I must have looked chagrined because she laughed. She had a sparkling quality, a rare vivacity that enchanted. "Don't worry, there are really not that many. Just the family, Richard Langley whom you've already met,

Clarice's friend, Anthony Richmond, and my husband's employer and his wife, the Grant Robertses. They more or less invited themselves. I think Mr. Roberts was curious as to what a lady architect would be like. Don't mind him; he's quite a boor."

We reached the doorway to the parlor. Mrs. Tyndall drew the folding doors aside and we went in. In spite of her reassurances, the room seemed filled with people. I made polite replies to her introductions as we moved about the gas-lit parlor.

Her sister, Clarice, looked a great deal like Mrs. Tyndall though she was thinner and a trifle sharp-featured. Nor did her welcome have the warmth of her sister's. She clung possessively to the arm of Anthony Richmond who surveyed me with a fixed and polite smile as he acknowledged the introduction. Knowing what he'd said about me likely being a war horse made me feel gauche and uncomfortable with him, and not a little hostile, although I laughed at myself for feeling so. He seemed a quiet enough young man but with a superior air that irritated me. His large dark eyes stared at me appraisingly, and I felt myself flushing, knowing all too well what he was thinking.

"Anthony is an architect, too, Miss Stewart," Clarice said coolly, "although my sister and her husband did not see fit to let him submit a design for their new house."

Mrs. Tyndall made an impatient motion with her hand. "Oh, Clarice, must you bring that up now? I've already explained to Anthony that our employing Miss Stewart was in no way a reflection on his talents. But his designs are on somewhat more of a regal scale than we want. As a professional person, he understands. I do wish you would."

Clarice merely sniffed, but Anthony, after a barely perceptible pause, smiled and bowed to Mrs. Tyndall. "Of course, Alice, don't worry about it." I thought him somewhat more attractive when he smiled. His teeth were even and white and contrasted with his deeply tanned face. I felt he must have spent a good deal of time out of doors to be tanned so late in October. His shoulders were broad, tapering to slim waist and hips but his hands were huge, too big, I thought, to handle delicate drafting tools. His hair was crisply brown and curling, beginning to recede a bit at the hair line. I wondered suddenly if he still thought me a war horse. Then I firmly put a check on my thoughts. What did I care what he thought of me? I had won a commission over his head, and he was understandably upset about it. If I were to survive in this profession, I would have to govern myself not to mind professional jealousy. So I smiled as nonchalantly as I could and extended my hand to him. "I am pleased to make your acquaintance," I said.

Mrs. Tyndall led me on to the Grant Robertses who were seated together on the couch. Mr. Roberts arose, almost grudgingly, as we approached. He seemed a pompous, humorless man from the cold, appraising way he fixed me with small, blood-shot eyes. He had fair, straight, slicked-back hair and a round, colorless face. I would have judged him to be no more than thirty-five but he was already inclined to corpulence.

"What on earth could induce a young woman like yourself to get mixed up in such an unwomanly racket as architecture?" he said abruptly, not even waiting for Mrs. Tyndall to introduce us. I could not help gasp at the bluntness with which he managed to insult me and our hostess by not allowing her to finish her introduction. I felt Mrs. Tyndall stiffen and heard her clear her throat preparatory to answering him. But I laid a restraining finger on her hand as it hung beside mine. After all, boor that he was, he was her husband's employer. I did not want her to have to defend me to him. But he was nothing to me, and I was getting quite good at defending myself.

"The good fortune to have been born with a talent for designing houses," I said, with deceptive sweetness. "I still can't believe my incredible luck."

Out of the corner of my eye I saw Anthony Richmond smile and, glancing quickly at him, caught a glint of approval in the dark eyes.

But the owner of the coal mine was not so easily silenced. He snorted almost angrily. "Seems downright indecent to me. Why don't you stay at home like any normal woman should?"

My anger flared in spite of my will to control it. Anger for myself, for the man's host and hostess, and for old Mr. Bosworth, who was standing near the doorway looking deeply distressed at such lack of manners being displayed in his home. It was his stricken face that quieted me. I stared at my tormentor's round, stupid face and did the only thing I could think of. I laughed and moved away.

Mrs. Tyndall, still trembling with outrage, presented me, then, to Mrs. Roberts.

She was a thin, rabbit-faced little woman who looked as though she might burst into tears. She murmured polite but hurried replies to Mrs. Tyndall's introduction and my greeting, her pale eyes darting toward her husband as if afraid he wouldn't approve of her speaking to me. I pitied her and smiled reassuringly as she threw me a look of mortification and apology for her husband's rude remarks.

My hostess quickly presented me to the others whom I had already met, though briefly; her brother, Jon, who leaned over and murmured a quick apology for Roberts' rudeness. "He's quite a savage, Miss Stewart. You handled him exactly right," he whispered. Richard Langley was there, too, looking elegant in a dark broadcloth suit and immaculate linen. He bowed over my hand and then straightened up, smiling down into my eyes. "You look lovely, Miss Stewart. No one would believe you'd had such a harrowing experience this morning." I thanked him and moved on to Mr. Bosworth.

The old man smiled and offered me his arm. "George is motioning me that dinner is ready," he said to the room at large. "I really can't understand what's keeping Mrs. Bosworth, but she would not want us to wait and spoil the goodness of the food. We'll go in, if you please." And with me on his arm, he led the way into the dining room.

It was a charming room with tall windows at one end and a black-marble fireplace like the ones in the parlors. Here, too, a gas log was burning, but the room was lit by dozens of candles. They flickered brightly in sconces on the walls and in great candelabra on the table and sideboard, their flames reflected in polished silver and crystal. George was standing behind the master's chair at the head of the table, and when he saw Mr. Bosworth, he pulled the chair out for him deftly with one hand, the chair at his right with the other. He made a quick motion of his head toward me to indicate that I was to sit there. Mrs. Tyndall sat at the far end of the table with the Robertses at either side of her. Clarice was beside Mr. Roberts, Anthony Richmond next to Mrs. Roberts across the table from Clarice and myself. Richard Langley took a place between Clarice and me while Dr. Jon sat at his father's left hand with Mr. Tyndall across from Langley between Jon and Anthony. I had the feeling the seating arrangement had been dexterously rearranged at the last minute by George. He smiled at me conspiratorially as if to confirm my suspicions. No doubt I'd been placed near Mr. Roberts and George, hearing the attack the man had made upon me in the parlor, had decided to remove me from his immediate proximity.

After Mr. Bosworth had said grace, Mr. Tyndall lifted his wine glass toward me.

"I propose a toast to Miss Stewart and to the wonderful house she'll build for Alice and me." He looked deliberately at Mr. Roberts and continued flatly, "I can't tell you all how fortunate we count ourselves to have her graciously agree to come here to Bellefonte for us. Alice and I will possess a true work of art when she has finished."

I flushed under his excessive praise, but basked under it, too. I was glad Mr. Tyndall was no sycophant of his employer. He seemed to be quite baldly saying the other man was insufferably rude and, moreover, quite wrong in thinking I should "stay at home." I thanked him as the others drank the toast, Mr. Roberts with the utmost reluctance, his wife just a shade behind him as if frightened to do so without his permission.

Mrs. Tyndall was a charming and accomplished hostess, which she had great need to be in such an assembly. Anthony Richmond seemed to be interested only in flattering Clarice, which he did frequently with sidelong glances at me as if, I thought, to say, "See how a gentleman treats a woman wise enough to stay out of competition with him?" And Mr. Grant Roberts rambled on in a monotone about means to improve production at his mine. Any attempts by Mrs. Tyndall to direct conversation toward a topic more congenial to everyone were met with his small-eyed stare. His wife sat silent and nervous, barely picking at the excellent food George served her.

I gathered from Mr. Roberts' monotonous droning that he and Mr. Tyndall had sharp differences about how the mine was to be run. He, the owner, counted everything in increased production and dismissed as molly-coddling nonsense some new safety precautions Mr. Tyndall was engaged in introducing. I wondered how a decent, humane man like my host could bring himself to work for such a robber-baron type, but it became apparent as he talked that he had insisted he be given complete control of the operation of the mine. Apparently, though Mr. Roberts deplored his safety innovations, production had increased dramatically under Mr. Tyndall, and so he was given his head, profits being the deciding factor in all Roberts' decisions.

"Were you aware that Mr. Tyndall is one of the world's foremost experts on mining?" Richard Langley said to me during an infrequent lull in Mr. Roberts' monologue. "He's written a number of books on the subject."

"Really? No, I didn't know that. How exciting," I said, smiling at Mr. Tyndall. "I'd like to read one of them, though I doubt if I'll understand a word."

He laughed. "You can if you want, they're in the library on the second floor. But my wife's books will be far more interesting, I'm sure. She's the real writer in the family."

I looked at Mrs. Tyndall in surprise. "You're a writer? How wonderful," I said. She surely was an astonishing and interesting woman. "What kind of books do you write?"

"Children's things mostly. A bit like the Elsie Dinsmore books. Only mine are for boys and girls, not just girls."

"When she isn't attending suffragette meetings," Clarice said disapprovingly, her slender nose quivering.

Jon frowned at his younger sister. "Clarice, try not to be disagreeable," he said softly.

She threw him a haughty stare. "Oh, Jon, don't play the big brother with me. Alice *does* make a spectacle of herself, forever pounding away at that ridiculous typewriter or picketing the courthouse for women to be given the vote. What a terrible embarrassment to Bill you are, Alice."

Mrs. Tyndall just laughed as if used to her sister's disapproval. But her husband threw her a warm smile. "She's no embarrassment to me, Clarice. She's my dearest inspiration," he said, with an air of deep satisfaction.

I stared at them almost wistfully. It *was* possible, I thought with sudden passion, for a woman to be something besides a household automaton and still retain the love and devotion of a fine man. The Tyndalls were living proof of it. How happy they seemed together. Mrs. Tyndall never waited for his approval before she expressed an opinion, as poor little Mrs. Roberts seemed always to do, yet he gazed at her with such admiration and respect while Mr. Roberts stared at his wife with barely concealed annoyance that she'd even dared to speak at all. And her few hesitant opinions, even when they coincided with his, seemed to arouse nothing but contempt in him.

But Clarice wouldn't leave it alone. "I still say she'd be better employed learning a few of the feminine graces in . . . how to please a man." She threw Anthony Richmond a languishing glance. He rose immediately to her obvious bait with a flattered smile.

"I suggest you conduct classes in those categories your-self, Clarice," he said gallantly.

She gave a little shriek of mock horror. "Thereby joining the women's work force? Oh, I beg you, don't consign me to such a fate. I can't *think* of anything worse."

I felt myself getting angry again, and before I could stop myself, I burst out, "I can. Going hungry."

She stared at me disdainfully. "Oh, I suppose some women *do* have to work," she conceded grudgingly. "But then, don't you think it would be better if they did something *feminine* like needlework or being a companion to an elderly gentlewoman?"

Mrs. Tyndall exploded. "Oh, for pity sake, Clarice, you are unbelievable. You've been lucky enough to be born with a silver spoon in your mouth. You don't know what it is to have to earn your way in life."

"*You* were born with a silver spoon in your mouth, too, darling. What's your excuse?" was the spiteful reply.

"I don't *need* an excuse," Mrs. Tyndall said. "I feel if one is lucky enough to have a talent, then it behooves one to use it. For good. I try to do that. But what I do isn't the point. We're talking about women who have to earn a living. It's extremely hard for them today, and I think you show a rare and ugly type of cannibalism that you would so criticize those of your sex for going out and supporting themselves instead of genteelly starving."

Mr. Tyndall spoke up spiritedly before his sister-in-law could reply. "Yes. For pity sake, take Mrs. Fuller over on Bishop Street. She's never had the opportunity to learn those 'feminine graces' you talk about, Clarice. When her husband died, leaving her with five children, she'd have been hard put to find a position as a 'gentlewoman's companion' or doing needlework in a small town where most women do their own. But the good soul didn't sit down to weep and let the town look after her brood. She put out a sign that she was available to do the very unfeminine chores of painting and hanging wallpaper."

"Yes, and what a scandal the woman is. She wears *trousers* to work," Clarice said in a horrified voice.

"Oh, mercy on us," her sister mimicked. "And that's worse by far than letting her children go hungry. I for one think she's a wonderful woman. And, if she wants the job, I'd like her to paper our new house."

Anthony Richmond smiled tolerantly. "All very well for poor Mrs. Fuller. As you point out, she's a brave and able little person and deserves all our admiration, no doubt. Better than the county having the children in the orphan's home. But after all, *she* has no man to take care of her. It's expected that she should do the best she can. But the natural function of women is to marry, thereby removing all necessity for them to work."

Surprisingly, Mrs. Roberts spoke up. "You wouldn't say that young man if you knew just how much work there is to the average household. Have you ever cleaned twelve rooms or done laundry for four children and a husband? And we just can't keep a day girl. They say we don't pay enough." She subsided suddenly, glancing quickly at her husband as if afraid she'd said too much.

He frowned in annoyance. "You'd not think housework so hard if you'd ever had to go out and fight for your bread in the marketplace, Emily. I've spared you all that."

She played with her fork, not looking at him, but everyone at the table could almost hear her thoughts. Was she all that lucky to have been "spared" earning her living?

"You're all missing the point," Mr. Tyndall said brusquely. "Of course married women who keep a house work. Harder, indeed, than many men today. So work, per se, isn't defeminizing. Why, do you know that the original meaning of the word 'lady' was that of a woman who provided for those who depended on her?"

"Exactly," his wife agreed.

"But there's nothing in the words God sent down from Sinai that says *how* a woman is to provide for her household. Or that she's a freak if she's able to do that which we call 'men's work.'"

Mr. Roberts put his hands down flat on the table with the air of one who'd been ignored just long enough. "Well, Tyndall, I can't say I approve of the way you live your personal life or of your unorthodox opinions," he said. "Fortunately your radicalism doesn't prevent you from being a good mine manager." He put a piece of bread into his mouth and continued speaking between smacking noises. "However, you might take a bit of advice from an older, wiser head. Give a woman your little finger, and she'll take your whole hand."

"Oh, *I* don't *give* my wife the privilege of writing or working for the franchise for women," Mr. Tyndall drawled. "God did that, you see. I just try not to succumb to the conditioning of years in expecting her to be my body slave."

Mrs. Tyndall's dark eyes gleamed wickedly. "So many times when men must act the slave master, it's only because they have grave doubts as to their own abilities," she said.

Mr. Roberts turned almost purple. He dabbed at his mouth with his napkin and even though I was thoroughly enjoying the verbal sparring, I began to think the Tyndalls had gone too far. Weren't they afraid of Mr. Tyndall being fired?

But before the mine owner could make a reply, George came into the room and cleared his throat. "Mr. Tyndall, there's some gennulmen here wants to see Mr. Roberts," he said.

"Show them in, George," Mr. Tyndall said with a hint of laughter in his voice.

As George went to conduct the newcomers in, Mr. Bosworth, who'd listened silently up until then, sighed and spoke with quiet pride. "You're quite right about women being talented beyond their natural abilities as wives and mothers, Alice," he said. "Your mother taught Jon all he knows about herbs and medicinals. Why old Dr. Blanchard used to say she was as good as he was any day."

"You're quite right, Father," Jon said. "In my own practice I often find myself asking myself, 'Now what would Mother do for the croup?' And you know, quite often her remedies are far more efficacious than the ones I find in the books. She spent a lifetime learning her healing arts."

"Where *is* Jenny?" the old man said querulously. "Oughtn't she to be back by now?"

George forestalled any replies by appearing in the dining room doorway with three coal-grimed miners on his heels.

The spokesman of the group, a burly man with eyes as brilliant-blue as agates in his blackened face, spoke peremptorily.

"We were told at your house you were here, Mr. Roberts," he said, "which made it convenient for us as we'd have come here next anyway."

"What's the meaning of interrupting a man's dinner?" Roberts said angrily.

"My son and the two Lafferty lads are trapped in number 5 mine. That's the meaning of it!" the man snapped angrily. "And the foreman wouldn't let us start digging for them without your okay. Oh, he's your stooge all right. Said he'd flatten the first man that started digging. Didn't want to chance a slide that would slow down production, for God's sake."

Mr. Tyndall stepped toward the men. "Get back out there right away, Tam, and tell that fool he's fired." He turned to Richard Langley. "Rick, you start through the town and get every off-duty miner you can find out to the mine. Tell them not to waste a second. George, get coffee brewed. Lots of it and make sandwiches."

The burly miner nodded. "I'll appreciate any help I can get. Even from you, Tyndall. But you're still Roberts' man in my book. You and your whole class. Feasting on miner's blood. If my son dies, I swear, every damned blood-sucking mine owner and manager and engineer in the company will pay for it."

And jamming his grimy hat back on his head, he whirled around and stalked from the room.

CHAPTER 3

If I should live to be ninety, I'll never forget that terrible night.

Mr. Tyndall and Richard Langley left immediately for the mine, but Mr. Roberts, pleading the necessity of seeing his wife home, declined to accompany them. Anthony Richmond offered to drive Dr. Jon there so that we could use the doctor's small rig to take food and coffee to the disaster scene. So, in very short order, the women and Mr. Bosworth were left alone with the servants who were working frantically to prepare food.

George wanted to go to the mine with Mrs. Tyndall, but she told him she'd far rather he stayed at home to look after her father and Annette. "Miss Stewart will accompany me, won't you?" she asked me and assumed my answer at the same time.

"Of course. I don't know much about nursing if it should be needed, but there'll be something I can do," I said.

She smiled approvingly. "Keeping coffee hot and ready and being there for the women to lean on a bit will be the most important thing."

Clarice was appalled. "You saw how that dirty miner attacked Bill, Alice. I think you're mad to go out there. It's their affair, not yours."

George stared at her disdainfully. "That gennulman

was jest upset about his son. Everyone in this town knows Mr. Bill is the miners' friend. Miss Alice is right. She *ought* to be there."

"If you think some women should be there, send Louise and Mary," she said with a gesture toward the two women who were piling sandwiches into a hamper and a large basket. "Think of how it looks, Alice."

Mrs. Tyndall exploded. "Sometimes I don't believe you're real, Clarice." Then, turning to George, "Get Mr. Jon's rig ready for us, please. I think both Miss Stewart and I had better change into something warmer."

We left the kitchen and hurried upstairs where I quickly found a heavy woolen skirt and sweater to wear under my winter coat and a pair of sturdy boots. A woolen scarf to tie about my head completed my needs, and I went out into the hall to meet my hostess who had two slickers, one for each of us.

"It's beginning to rain a bit," she explained. "Better put this on. It will be a long, uncomfortable night if you get wet."

By the time we reached the front porch, George had brought the buggy around and stowed the food and coffee under the seats.

"The big coffee pot's in there, Miss Alice," he explained. "An' the coffee. I also put in the crane we used to use to boil the maple sugar. There was no way I could make the coffee here and have you get it there without spillin' it all over everything. You sure you can manage? I'll be happy to come along."

"No, George, I feel better when you're with Father," she said. "Thanks for working so fast. We'll manage."

She flicked the reins and clucked at the horse, and we were off. "You know, those two old men sort of look after each other, but each thinks he's the one who does all the looking after," she remarked. "It's useful to be able to excuse them from doing things that are really too much for them by urging the other's need."

I smiled in the darkness. For all her forthrightness, Mrs. Tyndall had a delicate tact that endeared her to me. Yet, I remembered with amusement the heartless way she'd put Mr. Roberts in his place when his rudeness became unendurable. She and her husband were truly remarkable people. They had wasted no time in useless hand wringing, but had quickly and efficiently gone about doing the necessary things to help without even the need to consult each other.

"I hope Bill will be able to do something," she said abruptly. "I hope the men are just trapped by the cave-in and not crushed. Then, if the oxygen holds for a little while, there's a chance we can get to them."

There was really not much to say, so we drove the rest of the way in silence.

The disaster site was literally alive with people. Yet there was not the slightest sign of panic. There were several huge bonfires built to give light as well as warmth. The opening to the mine was at the base of a slowly ascending mountain, and men moved in and out of it with regularity. Dr. Jon explained that all the off-duty miners had been called, and they were taking turns digging away the fallen rubble at an old shaft about a hundred and fifty feet within the mine.

Already, Mr. Tyndall and Richard Langley had activated a gasoline-powered drill higher up on the mountain and were attempting to sink an air vent, fearing lack of oxygen would finish the miners before rescue attempts could succeed.

"Do . . . do they know if they're alive, Jon?" Mrs. Tyndall said softly, as she labored to erect the crane for her coffee pot over a smaller, cook fire that someone had started.

"Yes. Taps were heard," Jon said. "So someone is alive. Pray God we'll reach them in time. Look, Alice, yell if you need help. I've got to check over the medical supplies I brought along. The miners have erected a tent where we can get the men in out of the rain when they're rescued. Tony Richmond has gone back to town to get some cots and more blankets. I'll be right over there."

He strode off purposefully, his long legs taking impossibly huge steps. I liked the handsome, young doctor. It was easy to see that he was Alice Tyndall's brother.

We worked together, using a makeshift table two of the miners had erected for us from piles of logs with planks laid between. I marveled at what George and the two women had been able to do on such short notice. There were piles of ham sandwiches and a great bowl of hard-cooked eggs along with a huge crock of oatmeal cookies. He'd even packed a couple of dozen cups and a dishpan with soap and towels to wash and dry them as they were needed. There was coffee in a big jar and sugar in another with milk firmly sealed in bottles.

At the beginning of the night, the coffee pot was constantly being refilled, but no one wanted to eat. Later, when energies lagged and it became evident that a certain amount of time must go by until the men were rescued, they came silently as they finished their turn at the digging and ate.

The women and the children were heartbreaking. There were nearly as many women there as men, many with small children in their arms. They stood together, not speaking much, nor did I see any of them weep. It was as if doing so would acknowledge a reason for grief that they were in no way prepared to concede. Mrs. Tyndall pointed out the Lafferty boys' mother and Tam Whitney, the miner who'd come to the Bosworth house. Beside Tam stood a tiny dark-haired woman with a wide, motherly face. She held a little boy in each hand. They were handsome little fellows with eyes as blue as their grandfather's, for that's what Tam was to them, Mrs. Tyndall explained. They were his son's children, and since their mother had died the year before, Mrs. Whitney had been taking care of them.

"I pray their boy, Jim, is safe," she said solemnly. "They've already lost one son, Bill tells me, the younger boy, in the mine two years ago."

I stared at the little family achingly. What a hard lot the miners had digging away in darkness all their waking lives, knowing that at any moment a cave-in could end their lives or that lung diseases from the constant ingestion of the black dust could shorten their days. Hardly easier was the anxiety the women had to live with. When they kissed their husbands good-bye at the beginning of their shifts, none of them could be certain they'd be able to kiss them again at the end of it.

The drill above rattled on monotonously until after midnight when it finally broke through to the shaft where the miners were trapped. A faint halloo from below gave the welcome news that someone was alive to give it, and word quickly spread throughout the weary workers and spectators. A great shout of triumph rose from a hundred throats, and almost in the next moment the entire group had fallen to their knees to offer a prayer of thanksgiving.

Mr. Tyndall, now knowing that an air supply was assured the trapped men, came down to have a cup of coffee and a sandwich. Grant Roberts, the mine owner, still hadn't come to the scene. I thought his callousness abysmal. He was a caricature of a robber baron.

I remarked to Mrs. Tyndall about his seeming lack of concern for his employees.

"They're nothing to him except strong backs to dig the coal," she replied angrily. "He came here from New York after buying the mine, and he intends to return there as soon as Bill has taken over as manager. He hates Bellefonte and the people. I think they'll all be thoroughly glad when he leaves."

"I wondered how a fine man like your husband could bear to work for him," I admitted.

"*He'll* be glad to see Roberts go, too," she said, with a short laugh. "Actually, knowing he'd be given complete responsibility for the mine was what induced him to take the position. He and Mr. Roberts could never work together. They've already clashed over Bill's purchasing machinery like the drill up there that got air to the men in need. But by adding only fifty men to the crew, Bill was able to double production in the very first month. Mr. Roberts was even willing to pay for the drill when my husband got those results."

She sighed deeply. "Now this had to happen. What Mr. Whitney said was true, although it isn't Bill's fault. He's been systematically replacing aging and inferior timbers in the mine since he took over. Likely these lads were working in a part with the old timbers."

A new shift of workers came then for food and coffee and we broke off talking.

The spattering of rain that had been starting when we

left Bellefonte had turned to a persistent drizzle. I was glad for the slicker Mrs. Tyndall had offered me. The fires hissed and threw sparks, and some of the women took the smaller children into the medical tent to get them out of the rain. But still the rescuers dug on. There had been more intermittent tapping from within the mine and an indistinguishable voice through the air shaft. Thank God, the rescuers said, at least *one* of them is alive.

Suddenly, from the entrance to the mine, a tall miner came running, shouting and waving his arms. Then, as the sun's first rays crept above the pines, he loped across the clearing to where the women waited. I stood, unable to breathe, staring at the strained, anxious, suddenly hopeful looks on the tired faces and the unbearably poignant way Mrs. Whitney's fingers lay coiled in her grandson's hair. The miner went first to the Lafferty boys' mother, pulling his helmet from his head.

"They're alive, ma'am. Both alive and well, though Tom's got a broken arm that'll require care."

The woman's face worked against tears of relief. Then it turned as radiant as the sun that was rapidly dissipating the rain. "Thanks be to God," she cried brokenly, then the tears that had been held in abeyance throughout the long night began pouring down her face at last.

Mrs. Whitney stood with quiet dignity. As the miner turned to her, there was a subtle difference in his eyes, and although she could not have read his expression through the coal dirt on his face, she sighed deeply and reached a hand out to him as if in pity. "You needn't tell me, Jem, my lad's dead, isn't he?" she said softly. "Your eyes. They're the same as Logan Finnery's were when he came to tell us the other boy was dead."

"I'm sorry, Mrs. Whitney," the man said miserably. "I'd give all I got if I could say otherwise."

But before he could finish speaking, a great wail arose from the women. It broke the unnatural silence of the night and echoed off the brooding mountain face, making me think of ancient women mourning their men slain in battle. I felt tears rolling down my own cheeks though I didn't know these people. Yet their sorrow was mine. I felt a sisterhood with them, with all women who'd lost their men. Indeed, I thought suddenly, when a man had fallen in a glorious cause, at least his women might take some small comfort from that. How did they bear that his vigor should be crushed beneath a mountain? But even as I thought it, I felt there was a dignity greater than life in that. In a man going heroically each day to do unpleasant and dangerous work that those he loved might eat.

I felt rather than saw the Tyndalls behind me, and when I turned, they were staring at Mrs. Whitney with stricken faces, their hands clasped together as if to comfort each other.

Then, like some grim tableau, the women clustered about Mrs. Whitney and the two boys to offer her what comfort they could.

"Does . . . does Tam know?" she asked at last.

"Yes, ma'am. We tried to get him to come out to you when we found the Laffertys and they said Jim was buried farther back, but he wouldn't let up. Said he'd carry his own lad. They'll be coming now soon."

As he finished speaking, faint light from the mine adit proclaimed the miners' approach. They came trudging wearily out, two by two, one man with a hastily contrived sling on his arm. In spite of their sorrow, the spectators and off-duty miners cheered lustily at the appearance of the injured Lafferty boy and his brother. But their cheers soon died as the third miner was carried out in his father's arms.

Tam Whitney stalked across the clearing, staggering a little under his burden. His face was streaked with his own tears, but his eyes were cold with fury. He walked toward his wife and grandsons and almost ceremoniously, laid the crumpled body on the ground at their feet. The little boys began to sob bitterly, but Mrs. Whitney simply dropped to her knees and gathered the poor burden against her breast. I thought of a picture I'd once seen of Michelangelo's "Pietà." Though this woman was no passionate madonna and her son a poor coal miner, her sorrow was as deep and even more hopeless than Michelangelo's sorrowing mother's had been.

Tam Whitney stood staring down at his family, his fists clenched impotently at his sides. Then he caught sight of Mr. Tyndall standing behind Mrs. Whitney. He flew at him, striking out with his doubled fists.

"You bloody, damned murderer!" he screamed. "It was the timbers. The bloody, rotten timbers. How'd you expect rotting wood to hold up a mountain?"

Mr. Tyndall didn't lift an arm to defend himself. His face was twisted with pain and sympathy for the miner. But before the man could do more than land a couple of blows, his friends had grabbed him and held him in compassionate arms.

"Tam, Tam, it wasn't *his* doing. You know he's been replacing the timbers since he's taken over," pleaded the tall miner who'd brought the news of Jim's death. "Mr. Tyndall'd told the lads to steer clear of that tunnel till a crew replaced the timbers. You can't blame him."

"He's working for Roberts," replied the miner bitterly.

"What's one more dead miner to that lot? Build your new house, Tyndall. The mortar's mixed with miner's blood."

Mrs. Tyndall gasped in horror and clutched her husband's arm.

"God knows, you've grief enough that we can't hold you responsible for what you're saying, poor man. But Bill's not to blame for what happened. If he hadn't insisted on buying that drill, they might all have died before air could be gotten to them."

"Let him alone, Alice," Mr. Tyndall said steadily. "He needs to do something to relieve his grief. Let him say anything he wants."

"But he's wrong, Mr. Tyndall," said Tam's wife, releasing her son and gently covering his face with her shawl. "We all know how much better things have been since you've been here. It's his grief, as you said. It's hard for a man to lose both his sons in the mine."

Tam whirled on her furiously. "Oh, I'm unhinged now? Is that what you think, woman? Well, if I am, it's from living in a world where swollen mine owners can sit on their fat arses and grow rich while a poor man's sons go into the mines to sweat and die. They were your sons, too. Don't you have any feeling?"

She walked toward her husband and took his tortured face between her hands. "Come home with me, Tam," she said gently. "It's wrong for you to be screaming and brawling and accusing an innocent man over poor Jim's body. Come away home with me now. We've got to make arrangements. But first, we've got to pray a bit."

The poor man seemed to collapse against her all at once. He put his blackened hands up to hers, then drew her against him; it was hard to say who was leaning against the other the most. "Ah, Martha. We've lost them both, Martha. We've lost them both," he sobbed. "And you the best woman in shoe leather. How is it you should be tried so hard?"

She held him and comforted him as if he'd been one of the children who were sheltered in the arms of the other women now. "We've lost them. It's true. But to a better world than this one," she said, cherishing him. "You've often read me that bit in the Book about how God will wipe the tears from every eye. How there're many mansions for us all in heaven. Be my own good man, now. Buck up and think of our grandsons."

"I am thinking of them," he cried passionately. "What future is there for them except the one their father and uncle had?" He broke down again for a moment, then, pushing his wife back, whirled about to face Mr. Tyndall. "But if I have to sell my soul, they'll not! They'll never go into a mine to dig coal for another man."

Richard Langley stepped forward and touched Tam's arm. "This may not be the time to mention it, Whitney," he said gruffly, "but the lads won't have to mine. If you'll recall, Mr. Tyndall started an insurance program for the younger men when he came. Your boy signed up for it. There'll be money to send the little fellows to college."

"Is that supposed to make me stop hating him?" Tam cried unreasonably. "It's just a salve to his conscience. And I'll believe it when I see it."

His wife threw Mr. Tyndall a look of mingled sorrow and apology.

"He's ill with his grief. Let me get him home," she said, drawing her husband along with her. "He'll bless you and thank you for it in time as I do now, sir."

They turned and helped each other off toward the row of miners' homes down the valley. Slowly the others

picked up the body of the dead boy and moved off toward their homes, leaving us, the townspeople, the outsiders, alone.

Mrs. Tyndall squeezed her husband's hand. "Don't
mind, my darling," I heard her whisper. "It's grief. It can
make a man mad."

It was nearly mid-morning before we returned to the
Bosworth home, only to find the entire household in an up-
roar.

George had gone to awaken his employer when he
didn't come down for breakfast. The old gentleman was
gone, his bed not slept in. Now Mary was frantically
searching the house, even going up into the glass-
enclosed widow's walk where, George said, Mr. Bosworth
had spent much time looking out over the mountains for
his wife when she'd first disappeared. He'd even looked in
the old hidden room, he declared, finding no trace of Mr.
Bosworth. His jacket and hat and walking stick were
gone, too, making them think he'd gone off somewhere.

"Calm down, all of you," Mr. Tyndall commanded.
"Are you sure he didn't just get up and go for a walk before you, George?"

"Ain't likely, sir. I been up since five. Been thinkin'
'bout them poor miners. Did you get them out okay?"

"Two of them, George. Jim Whitney was dead, I'm
sorry to say," Mr. Tyndall answered.

Clarice came down from a further search through the
bedrooms, looking flushed and beautiful for all her agitation. "You *know* Father never gets up before eight-thirty,
Bill. And in my whole life, I've never known him to make
his bed. Why would he have done so this morning? He
must have gone out last night after I retired. He said he'd

be right up, but I was tired and fell asleep quickly. He hadn't come up by then."

"Then, I suppose we'd better get a search organized immediately," Mrs. Tyndall said, with a tremor in her voice. I looked at her quickly. She was pale and seemed tired but she was very much in command of herself. I knew that if she felt as weary as I did, she was near to swaying on her feet.

"George," Mr. Tyndall said, "get the sheriff on the line. Tell him what's happened. I hope there'll be a few men left in town not too tired to go out. Nearly everyone was at the cave-in."

Annette, who'd been sitting on the sofa, weeping quietly, ran forward and threw herself into her mother's arms.

"He'll never come back. It'll be just like Grandma," she sobbed.

George stared at the little figure in dismay. "S'all my fault. Miss Alice trusted me to look after him. I should have stayed up with him. I was cleaning up in the kitchen and getting things ready to make breakfast to take to the mine in case the gennulmans wasn't found yet. I should have seen for myself that he'd gotten to bed all right."

"Now both of you stop that this minute," Mr. Tyndall said sharply. He knelt down and took Annette away from her mother. "We will find your grandad, Annette. I promise you," he said solemnly, looking into her eyes. "Now you go upstairs and turn down his bed. Have Mary keep a brick hot to warm it when you see us coming. He'll be cold and tired. Then you come back down here and do everything you can to help George and the girls. Do you understand?"

"Yes, Dad. I'll do as you say," she said, gulping down

her tears and going toward the stairs. She turned and looked at us, especially singling out her father before she mounted them. "I know you'll find him, Dad. It can't happen twice. I know you'll find him."

"Good girl. Just keep thinking that and don't be afraid."

We quickly drank the coffee George had left on the back of the stove. It was strong and bitter now from sitting so long, but it revived us and helped wash down the cold breakfast Mr. Tyndall insisted we all eat. By the time we were ready to set out searching the woods and mountains near the house, the sheriff and most of the men who'd kept vigil at the mine the night before, including Anthony Richmond, Jon Bosworth, and Richard Langley, had arrived. Even Grant Roberts was with the group this time, although it didn't appear he intended to take part in the search for he was dressed in a pale gray plaid suit and white spats.

The sheriff quickly organized the men into search parties, sending them off in different directions with instructions to fire a pistol, which he supplied to the accomplished woodsman he'd put in charge of each group, should Mr. Bosworth be found, as a signal to the other groups to come in.

Mrs. Tyndall turned to me suddenly. "Listen, Miss Stewart, I can't stand this waiting here. I've got an idea where Father might be. There's an abandoned quarry near here. Years ago, they drilled through to an underground spring that flooded it, making it impossible to get any more rock from the place. When I was small, Father and Mother used to take us there often for picnics. I wonder if he mightn't have gone there. I'm going to go see. Would you like to come along?"

"Yes. Of course. Anything will be better than just waiting."

We set off in a northeasterly direction up Curtin Street. My companion's face was strained from her long night at the mine, but she walked briskly. We passed several large homes, somewhat isolated on large lots with woods and meadows in between, then, finally, we were on a mere wagon track with only wilderness around us.

She turned off the track to the left and started down a slight slope toward the mountain range that formed one side of the long valley where Bellefonte nestled. There was a gap in the mountain at this point which afforded a view of other mountain ranges off to the west, purple and undulating, the nearer ridge and gap a multi-colored frame of elm and maple and oak.

"How beautiful!" I exclaimed, stopping for a moment in sudden admiration in spite of my concern for Mr. Bosworth. "What a spectacular view."

She smiled absently, her eyes searching the meadow below us as it fell sharply to a copse of trees at the base of the mountain. "Yes. The view is the principal reason we bought the land. A hundred acres of it. And this is where I want our house to stand."

"Oh, what a site!" I said excitedly. "What a lovely place to build a house."

"You'll do it full justice, I know," she said as we started down the slope. "My goodness. So much has happened since you arrived I'd almost forgotten the reason." She reached out impulsively and touched my arm. "You've been like one of us in our troubles. As if you've lived here all your life. Would you mind if we called you Minerva? And would you call us by our first names, too?"

"Oh, I'm so glad you said that," I said warmly. "I feel

honored that you want me to. And I feel the same way—
that I've lived here all my life, I mean. Which is strange
considering I'm a city girl."

"Not at heart," she said, with a smile.

We forded a mountain stream where crystal-thin ice
clung to rocks at wide places where the water lay in
pools. I shivered as I looked at it, thinking of Mr. Bosworth, frail and elderly, out in these cold mountains
throughout the night.

"The water is unbelievably cold," Alice Tyndall said,
as if she read my thoughts. "Most of the water in the
county is from mountain springs. It's where the town got
its name, in fact. The French statesman, Talleyrand,
while he was in exile in America, visited the home of
James Harris, one of the co-founders of the town. They
showed him the huge spring that supplied the entire area
with water. Indeed, it still does. The legend goes that
Talleyrand exclaimed, 'La Belle Font' in great admiration.
Mrs. Harris, recognizing a neat appellation when she
heard one, proposed that the new settlement be named
Bellefonte. That was late in the eighteenth century."

We were ascending a rough wagon track which wound
up and around the hill below the Tyndalls' house site. She
explained that it had been an access road to the quarry in
the old days and approached it from branch-offs at several places. It was now ankle deep with crisp, many-
colored leaves, its banks lined with scarlet sumac. The
sun was growing stronger by the minute waking sluggish
katydids to play a mournful dirge to the end of summer.

We came out on the top of the ridge, wind-swept and
beautiful.

"This is the highest point above the quarry," Alice said,
as she led the way, "we can see down into it from here.

Be careful, though. It's a terrible drop. A hundred feet to the water, at least."

In spite of her warning, I gasped in a sort of primitive spasm as we came abruptly to the edge of a deep, perfectly perpendicular chasm. The quarry was an enormous cut into sheer rock, as if a giant had carved the center out of a great, white cake. The walls where we stood dropped away as if they'd been cut with a plumb line. They were not quite so steep on the far side of the quarry, some three hundred feet away, and both sides sloped downward sharply to our left so that at the very end, one could approach the green, green water that filled the chasm almost from a mere ledge.

"It's so cold," my companion said bleakly. "There've been drownings here, even in mid-summer, when swimmers chilled and cramped from the cold. It's so deep, you see. At least as much space below the surface of the water as there is here above it. If my father stumbled into it in the night . . ." Her voice broke and she put her hand to her mouth but she kept searching the surface of the water bravely with her eyes.

"Don't think about that," I commanded. "He's not here. You could easily see if he had fallen in."

She smiled wanly, and there was relief in her eyes as she finished her scanning of the surface and turned toward me. "Yes. Thank God he isn't here. Now there's still hope. This was the first place I looked when Mother disappeared, too."

"Let's look around on the other side," I suggested, as much to get myself away from the edge of the eerily beautiful quarry as to distract her. "There are thick pines up that way. He might have taken cover somewhere away from the rain last night. That would afford some protection."

"You go that way, I'll move around the rim to the left. We can meet at the far side, thus covering more ground. But don't wander far from the quarry or you might get lost. The mountains can be deceptive."

I nodded and started off to our right toward the copse of pines. She had no need to worry about me venturing far; I was too much afraid of getting lost in the strange terrain.

The pines were so thick that it was hard to tell the sun was now shining brightly. Beneath the trees, footfalls were hushed by thick deposits of pine needles; there was a timeless, protected gloom. I found myself peering, breath bated as if it was an intrusion on my part to even be here, in the dark recesses of the copse. Shadows seemed to move and waver off, and the silence almost seemed to be that of someone waiting, watching me. Indeed, so charged did the stillness become that I felt certain someone *was* there in the depths, just out of sight, perhaps. I started to venture deeper into the thick woods, then remembered Alice's caution about getting lost. I called out, then.

"Mr. Bosworth, are you there?" but there was no answer. Only the feeling, irrational and primeval, that I was being watched. I was suddenly afraid. If Mr. Bosworth were in there, why didn't he answer my call?

I backed toward the edge of the copse of trees suddenly aware that my only line of retreat lay along the precipice unless I risked getting lost by moving farther into the deep woods to my right or left. It was foolish to think I could be of use in this area. I'd find Alice and get searchers who were familiar with the forests. Already I was as frightened as a child and imagining all sorts of ogres.

A dark figure seemed to waver insubstantially against the darker backdrop of trees almost as if called from my own uneasy imagination. I felt my heart accelerate its cadence as a fear I couldn't explain took possession of me.

"Mr. Bosworth?" I said fearfully.

The figure didn't answer but seemed to come fearsomely on toward me. I turned and ran, then, blindly back toward the narrow path along the edge of the quarry. Behind me I felt rather than heard sudden pursuit in the ankle-deep pine needles.

Just then I heard a gun shot farther down the valley. A bare moment later, Alice came running through the high grass toward me. We met in the middle of the clearing. Her face was filled with hesitant hope.

"They've found him," she breathed. "Oh, I pray God he's all right."

She seized my hand and began running with me back toward the upper end of Curtain Street. I looked back over my shoulder at the thick hemlock woods. There was no sign of a pursuer.

I laughed shudderingly in a spasm of emotional relief. The dear old man had been found! Suddenly I realized how much of a strain I'd been under since my arrival in Bellefonte. The thick, dark woods had played on my exhausted nerves until I was actually imagining shadows to be assailants. Here in the bright sunlight as I raced hand in hand with Alice Tyndall to her father, I felt shamefaced about my nervousness. I was certainly acting like a city girl all right. I was glad that Alice Tyndall with her high courage and unshakeable confidence had not witnessed my cowardice.

Mr. Bosworth proved to be suffering from nothing more than a mild case of exposure. He was a very strong man in spite of his seeming frailty, and fortunately, had been well dressed against the elements. He'd been found by Bill Tyndall wandering not a mile from the house, quite lucid and on his way home after a night of watching and calling for his wife. For the moment, he was aware again that she was missing and likely dead.

But, as Bill Tyndall pointed out, there'd likely be another time. The whole family would have to be aware of that. For his own sake, Mr. Bosworth would need to be watched carefully.

CHAPTER 4

Once assured that Mr. Bosworth was none the worse for his night in the woods, I for one slept until noon.

The rest of the house was still silent as I got up and drew a bath. Annette had been allowed to stay home from school, of course, and there was silence even from her room. I dressed quietly and gathered up sketch pads and pencils, thinking I'd walk up Curtin Street and make some preliminary sketches of the terrain and perhaps even work on ideas for the house itself. I wrote a note telling the family where I was and went downstairs, intending to put it on the hall table. But Jon, hearing my footsteps on the stairs, came in from the kitchen, coffee pot in hand.

"You should still be in bed, young lady," he said in a mildly chiding manner. "I'm sure several more hours of sleep would not come amiss for you."

"*You're* up and about," I countered, coming the rest of the way down the stairs.

He laughed good-naturedly. "I want to check on my patient again." Then, with an inviting motion of the coffee pot, "Come on out and have some scrambled eggs with me. That's the only dish I'm the master of."

"Sounds fine. I *am* hungry." I put my note on the table and followed him down the long hall to the kitchen.

"The maids have gone marketing, and George is upstairs in Father's room. I can't get him to go to his own. He's moved a cot into Father's room. Says that's where he'll stay from now on. I suppose there'll be a real donnybrook when Father wakes up."

"I'm so glad everything turned out well. You've all been through so much. And your poor father. I hope he soon gets over his doubts and confusions about your mother's fate. It must be terribly wearing on him."

He frowned and turned the eggs out onto two green-and-white plates, adding chunks of bread he'd toasted on a fork over the open flame from the cook stove. I got up and poured coffee from the agate pot, then buttered the toast.

"Yes. I wish I knew what to do. I confess, his condition is beyond my sphere of knowledge. There is a man named Freud in Austria who is beginning to study the human mind, trying to learn what makes it malfunction periodically and how its health and vitality can be restored. But he's only just beginning. Up until now, medicine has concerned itself with treating ailing bodies but considered ailing minds as some sort of personal weakness, or worse, the results of 'sin.' I don't really know what to do to help Father face reality. My good common sense tells me that if he'd actually *seen* her body, shattering as the experience would have been for him, he wouldn't now be suffering from these periodic delusions that she's still alive and wandering out there."

"That makes sense. Uncertainty about anything can be very hard on a person," I said.

"As it is now, I doubt if he ever truly grasps that she's gone. He doesn't talk about it for days on end, then suddenly, he's back to staring from the widow's walk or pacing the floor worrying that something has happened to her." He threw his hands outward in a sudden helpless gesture. "I feel so helpless. What good is all my training if I can't help my own father in his illness?"

"Perhaps one day her body will be found. The hunting season is starting. There'll be many people in the woods again. It seems impossible that there's never been a trace."

"Yes. It's very strange. But in these wilds she may *never* be found," he said bleakly. "So, I've been following this Freud's work carefully, trying to find a solution." He stood up and began carrying our dishes to the tin sink in the corner of the kitchen.

I finished my coffee and rose to help him. "Jon, you go see to your patient, I'll clear up here. Where's the dishpan?" I said.

He showed me where things were and pulled on his jacket.

"Listen, Minerva, if you're not too tired this evening, how about going to the new opera house with me. There's a performance of *The Planter's Wife* starring Katie Rhodes opening this evening."

"Really? I saw her once in Philadelphia."

He laughed spontaneously. "And your face tells me you're surprised to find her here in the hinterlands. Don't be. We have a very fine opera house. The best performers come here regularly and, it seems, are deeply gratified by the fine appreciation Bellefonte's citizens have for the arts."

"I'm beginning to see that Bellefonte has everything," I said teasingly. "Its people seem to think it's next door to heaven."

He smiled warmly. "Now that you're here, I'm inclined to agree with them."

"That's a very gallant remark and I'll be delighted to go to the theater with you," I said lightly, wishing I could conceal the flush that I felt flowing up my cheeks at his compliment.

"I see you're prepared to do some sketching," he said, indicating my materials which I'd left on the end of the kitchen table.

"Some preliminary house sketches. I can't wait to get something down on paper," I said.

"I don't know why they're so blamed anxious to build a house," he said, with sudden vehemence that startled me. "This one will be theirs in time anyway."

I looked up quickly at the anger in his voice. His statement surprised me to say the least and left me oddly embarrassed, too. My face must have betrayed my feeling for he laughed oddly and said, "Oh, they don't know it, you see, but Father's willed this house to Alice, one down on Spring Street which he owns to Clarice, and the money to be divided between them."

"What about you?" I couldn't help blurting, then ducked my head to hide my dismay.

"Oh, I'm a man," he said ironically, "with the best education money could buy, so Father thinks he's done well enough by me."

"I'm sure if your sister and brother-in-law knew about it, they'd prevail upon your father to consider you in his will. Especially since you seem to be the one who looks after him the most."

He shook his head. "No. He's quite set in his ways about it. Feels men were born strong to make their own way while women are tender little flowers to be cherished and provided for by the men in their lives."

I shook my head unbelievingly. "I realize I'm speaking

out of turn, but that seems most unfair to me. *You* will be the one expected to care and provide for some other woman, whereas Alice already has a strong well-to-do husband and her own considerable talent to rely on. Even Clarice, while not as self-sufficient as your older sister, seems likely to have a prosperous man marry her," I said, thinking of Anthony Richmond.

"I know. But, as you can see, I'm in the difficult position of not wanting to seem to question my father's right to do as he pleases with his money. Moreover, demanding anything for myself would seem to be grasping at what my sisters will have." He laughed mirthlessly and shook his head. "So, I'm caught in this old chivalry trap that's part of the culture we live in."

"I'm sure your sisters will treat you fairly when the time comes," I said reassuringly. "Alice could sell you the house for a token amount, perhaps. Or Clarice."

"Alice, yes. Clarice, I'm not so sure," he said, with a twinkle in his eye. "At any rate, I don't waste time worrying about it."

"You know, I'm surprised your father hasn't told Alice that she's to have this house," I said speculatively, "since he so would like to have them stay on here. Might it not influence their decision to build?"

"You'd lose a job," he said teasingly.

"Yes," I agreed, "and I certainly can't afford to, but it does seem a shame that Alice doesn't know about all this. I feel she might influence your father to be more realistic."

"Don't you tell her. Father would never forgive me."

"How is it that you know about it and the girls don't?" I asked.

He threw back his head and laughed. "Would you be-

lieve it? He made *me* executor." Still laughing, he took his
hat from a peg behind the kitchen door and picked up his
black bag. "I'll see you tonight, Minerva. Have a good
day," he said as he left the room.

In a little while I heard the front door shut as he went
out. I emptied the dishpan and refilled it with hot, soapy
water, washing and rinsing the dishes quietly. What Jon
had told me about his father's will troubled me in a vague
way. I had been only too painfully aware for several years
now that the way the world considered women was really
detrimental to them. All the gallantry that kept life
smooth for them also enslaved them in many instances.

For the first time, I understood how difficult it was for
men. If Jon's sisters had been brothers, he'd never have
stood by so peaceably while their father ignored his
needs. But they were women, weak and helpless, and so
must be protected from any unpleasantness at any cost. I
knew that he loved his father dearly. But yet, he must
surely resent the old man's misguided chivalry. The girls,
both married to wealthy men, would inherit money and
houses that would be superfluous while Jon, who only too
often had to take payment in eggs or potatoes for his professional services, would be lucky to be able to make a
living. I wondered that he could accept it with such equa-
nimity.

Sketch pads in hand, I walked up the rough wagon
track that was Curtin Street. The countryside was even
more beautiful now in early afternoon. The sun was
strong and warm, making me feel languorous. Likely I'd
fall asleep the moment I sat down to sketch.

I came to the spot on Curtain Street where the house
would stand. I was glad they'd chosen the spot where the

break in the mountain showed the panorama beyond. Today, the hills seemed to stretch off toward every dream I'd ever known. The land about me hummed with a strange, contented song of life. How wonderful just to sit here and stare off at the everlasting hills. I did just that for a long time, enjoying the sun on my back, feasting my senses on the Pennsylvania hills and knowing contentedly that the long valley at my back was dozing peacefully in the sun. The Happy Valley, the people called it, and a happy place for me despite the problems that had beset me during my time here.

And I could readily envision the house I would build for the Tyndalls. I felt a surge of deep satisfaction that I should be the one who designed the home they'd share. They were so happy together and loved each other devotedly, making for their child a warm nest of love and security. I was delighted to know that the walls I conceived would shelter their lives. Deeply moved by my own slightly wistful thoughts, I picked up my pencil, then, and taken out of myself as I had never been before by the creative process, I began making rapid sketches.

During our discussion in Philadelphia, I'd gotten some idea of what the Tyndalls wanted. They had pointed out the things in my designs that had especially appealed to them, so I was fairly sure they would like what I was doing. They'd insisted there be at least ten rooms, which had somewhat surprised me knowing they had only one child. But Alice had laughed and said they were confident they'd have many more children and she wanted to be prepared for them. Moreover, they had many friends from Philadelphia and they wanted to have room to entertain them. Indeed, she'd added graciously, she hoped that I'd consider myself one of them.

The magnificent view, of course, was the primary attraction of the land, that and the comparatively level terrain, rare in hilly Bellefonte which had been built on a little mound of hills in the center of the Nittany Valley. Someday, Bill Tyndall had said, the town would expand out this way. Sale of lots on either side of the spacious one he'd laid out for their house would be an addition to his childrens' fortunes. Nor would other homes being built below their house in any way detract from their own view for the land sloped gently but steadily down in the back so that when other streets should be laid out, all would share the view without interfering with anyone else's.

I sketched for an hour, loving the house that emerged beneath my pencil as if it had been a darling child. It should have dutch gables so that the third floor would consist of roomy chambers and not sharply pitched and useless attic space. Storage needs would be met in large closets throughout and in the high dry basement which, on the sloping lot, would walk-out to the rear. There would be four bedchambers on the second floor. The master bedroom would sit in the middle of the house, commanding a view through wide windows of the mountains. Thus, Alice Tyndall could readily check on those children she confidently expected. Four more spacious rooms on the third floor would be ready for the guests that meant so much to them. Each room would be well lighted and have privacy from the others. One would serve as a library-bedroom, perhaps for Annette.

The stairs I placed in a towerlike addition to the right of the front door which entered the front hall at a "cattycorner" angle. The stairs would take very little space from the floor plan but would ascend all the way from cellar to the third floor in a series of landings. Bill Tyndall had told

me there was a remarkably pretty yellow pine that grew
only in central Pennsylvania. I had seen samples of it in
the Bosworth house. From this I would build the staircase, a sunny accent in this happy house. Yellow and
warm and deeply grained, rustic rather than formally elegant as walnut was. And I would use native materials on
the outside, too. The snowy white limestone used in many
of the houses on Linn and Allegheny streets would dramatically accent the house as it stood silhouetted against
the mountains from which the stone came.

On the first floor, the large entrance hall would become
a part of the octagonal shaped dining room when the slid-
ing doors between were open, making the entire center of
the house, with the stairs in the tower, look like a medieval great hall, open and welcoming to the guests. Indeed,
the corner fireplace that formed one of the octagonal
corners of the dining room added to the great-hall feeling.
A massive corner cupboard would form the other corner
on the front end while windows across the entire rear
wall, catty-cornered at the ends would make the room a
perfect octagonal.

The front hall, too, would have a fireplace, kept glowing with coal for warmth and welcome, as would be the
one in the center inside wall of the parlor. The three fireplace openings would form a triangle, all utilizing the
same chimney. All around the parlor, with french doors
opening onto it from either end, would be a wide sunny
porch so that the inhabitants of the house could enjoy the
view of valley and mountains from three sides at all hours
of the day. But there'd be no costly roof to be kept up.
The second-story rooms would be built out over the porch
so that the second story would be bigger than the first.
The result was a large but compact house, its walls form-

ing roughly a square, built upward so that every inch of space was usable, having a purpose. I sketched rapidly, realizing I had room for an auxiliary pair of stairs in the tower beside the cellar entrance so that one could get to the second floor landing from the kitchen as well as the front hall, a step saver for the lady of the house and a means of keeping the children from wearing out the front-hall carpeting.

I sat back, drawing diagonal lines on some of the smaller windows. They'd be leaded, adding more to the medieval look. I was pleased with it and as exhausted with its creation as if I'd walked ten miles.

Suddenly, a shadow fell across my sketch pad. I whirled around, clutching the precious drawings protectively. Anthony Richmond was standing just behind me, staring down at my sketches, a sardonic smile on his swarthy face.

"You frightened me out of a year's growth," I said accusingly. "I didn't hear you approach."

"I *am* sorry," he said blandly. "I was just taking a bit of a breather from a house I'm working on the next street away. Beyond the trees there on Linn Street."

I composed myself quickly, instinctively covering my sketches with my hat.

"I can't imagine why you were so terribly frightened," he said as if he barely concealed amusement at me.

"I was *not* frightened, I was startled," I said untruthfully for, indeed, I had been shudderingly aware just for a moment, that I was not all that far from the copse of trees above the quarry where I'd thought I'd seen someone lurking.

He smiled down at me as if not totally convinced of my veracity, then sank down on the dried grass beside me, deliberately reaching for my sketch pad. "May I?" he said ironically, I thought, since he'd already taken possession of the drawings.

"They are rough yet, you understand," I said, hating myself for immediately feeling defensive.

"Of course," he said. I didn't think he meant it reassuringly, but rather as if he'd expected nothing else from me but rough, unfinished work. I bit the inside of my cheek, furious with him and with myself for letting his superior manner irritate me.

He perused my drawings in silence, his dark eyes intent on the pages, a faint smile on his lips. Watching him, hating myself for caring what he thought of them, I waited for his first comment. But he merely put them back down on the grass between us.

"What do you think of them?" I asked, seething inwardly for even asking him.

"You've got every type of architecture I've ever seen except Egyptian and Greek," he said complacently. "I *didn't* notice anything resembling a pyramid in the drawings."

How insufferably rude he was! I gathered my sketches quickly and began to stand up. "Oh, I was certain *you'd* not like them," I said.

"I didn't *say* I didn't like them," he answered reasonably. "But you must admit, they're a hodgepodge of design."

"Maybe so. I have never claimed to be one of those architects who blithely copy only colonial or federal or gothic."

"No, you seem to copy them all."

"I do not. I simply take what's best from every period and use it in my own design."

"The result is a virtual Frankenstein of architecture."

I could have slapped him. In fact, my palm ached to connect with his superior smile. It was as though he'd labeled my *child* a monstrosity. "What would *you* have designed for the Tyndalls?" I snapped. "A Victorian mausoleum like that *thing* you're doing downtown? Oh, I saw it. Mr. Bosworth pointed it out the day I came. Said the architect was a friend of the family."

"As a matter of fact, no. Likely I'd have done something on the scale you're planning here. But I'd have steered clear of some of the innovations you have."

"Like what?" I demanded.

"Like that porch. Better to have a more spacious living room than all that porch space."

"It will be an outdoor living area for them six months out of the year," I said defensively.

"And why would you have all the windows opening to the back? The street's the place to have windows opening onto."

"Why? So the owners can peer at their neighbors from behind heavy draperies they've erected to keep their neighbors from peering at them?" I stormed. "No, the Tyndalls aren't like that, and I know they love the view of the mountains. *That's* why the house has most of the windows opening to the back."

"Can you explain the need for *three* laundry tubs in the basement?"

"Ask any woman. Because some clothes need to soak while others are being washed. Because, often, when a child is covered with sand or mud, a mother would welcome a warm place she could bathe him without lugging him dripping dirt all the way to the bathtub on the second floor. Because in most households, a woman spends more time washing clothes than in any other chore. These tubs will all have water running into them and drains so that Alice won't have to lift any buckets of water for rinsing clothes."

"The woman's touch in architecture," he said sarcastically.

"What's wrong with that? It's a woman who spends her life taking care of a house, doing the work that a family entails. It's high time men consulted them about the houses they build."

"It will look ridiculous. Dutch gables, towers, leaded-glass windows. You've got too many periods."

"They're harmoniously blended into the whole. That's what good design is." I whirled about and started to walk away from him. But he got up swiftly, and gallantly taking my sketch pads walked alongside me.

"I suppose you'll be entering the blamed house in the *American Architect and Builder*'s contest for a modern American home," he said, referring to a well-publicized promotion by a leading magazine.

"I hadn't considered it. But I'm grateful to you for mentioning it," I said shortly. "Perhaps I will."

He grinned ruefully. "I shouldn't have mentioned it. I've entered a design myself. Perhaps you'll beat me."

"Oh, how could that ever be?" I said sarcastically. "My house is a hodgepodge and will please no one but the woman who's going to live in it."

"I didn't say that, either," he said reluctantly. "Why do you have to get so defensive about everything? If you're serious about being a professional woman, you'd better darned well develop a thicker skin."

"Oh, I can see that's a necessity, all right," I chaffed,

"to protect one from the barbs male competitors like to hurl."

"All of which simply supports my contention that women are in no way cut out for pursuing careers. You take purely professional criticism personally. You react emotionally to everything. Indeed, why don't you admit you'd be happy to settle down and be some man's wife if the opportunity presented itself."

I snatched my sketch pads out of his hands and to my complete surprise, hit him over the head with them. Then, ashamed of my temper, I burst into tears and turned and ran away from him. I could hear him laughing in his insufferably superior manner behind me. Why, oh why had I allowed him to goad me into such an action? I had proved that all his theories about women pursuing careers were true. At least in his eyes.

As I got out of sight of Anthony Richmond, I slowed down to a brisk walk, struggling to compose myself. It wouldn't do to come bursting into the Bosworth home with tears rushing down my flaming cheeks. I could just see Clarice's smug, hypocritical smile if I did so. Not that she wouldn't hear about the encounter anyhow. I was quite sure Anthony Richmond would tell her, dwelling with delight on every detail of my thorny performance.

A horseman was coming up Allegheny Street as I reached the corner a block above the Bosworth house. I saw that it was Richard Langley. He dismounted and took his hat off as he walked toward me, leading his horse.

"What a pleasant surprise, Minerva," he said, for somehow, during all the drama of the mine cave-in and Mr. Bosworth's disappearance, we'd all managed to get on a first-name basis. "I was just on my way to the Bosworths to call on you and ask if you were quite recovered from the events of the past two days. And, of course, to inquire after Mr. Bosworth."

"He was still sleeping when I left two hours ago," I said. "Jon felt he was quite well. As for me, as you can see I am none the worse for my adventures."

He smiled warmly; his deep-blue eyes crinkling at the corners. He was an exceptionally handsome man with a quiet courtliness that made him seem very appealing to me after Anthony Richmond's bland superiority. "I see you've been sketching," he said. "Plans for the new house?"

"Yes. I got more done today than I'd have dared expect," I replied, grateful for a chance to calm down before I entered the Bosworth house. "I hope the Tyndalls will like what I've done."

"I'm sure they will," he said. "I suppose, if things went so well, you'll be breaking ground quite soon."

"Not really. I think it will be spring before we start. Not only because the weather will be turning bad soon but because there will be a great deal to do. These are only preliminary drawings. Sketches, really. If the Tyndalls approve of them, then my real work will begin. Blueprints, material specifications, dickering with suppliers."

"Oh, will you be doing the contracting, too?"

"No. But I'll work closely with the builder until I'm sure all the materials I want in the house are available. For instance, where I've specified white limestone I think it would spoil the overall design if the builder were to substitute, say, red brick."

"That isn't likely to happen in Bellefonte. We've a

munificence of white limestone," he said with a smile. "It seems you have quite a job cut out for you. I don't know much about architecture, but I imagine it's quite as fascinating as mining engineering."

"That's a loaded statement. I must confess, engineering never had much fascination for me, although the fields are related at least in a superficial way."

"Will you have the facilities to work here?" he asked as we reached the front door of the Bosworth house. "I mean, don't you require big drafting tables and things like that?"

"I'm using Mr. Bosworth's library. He's kindly moved his desk out of the way, and Bill has borrowed the necessary tables." I thought with sudden pique that he'd likely borrowed the table I'd be using from Anthony Richmond's firm.

I opened the front door and stepped into the foyer. "I suppose Mr. Bosworth will be awake by now if you'd like to see him for a moment," I said, remembering that he'd come to inquire after the old man's condition.

He shook his head and twisted the horse's reins about his hand, preparatory to mounting. "No, I've had a long day at the mine. I really want a good meal and a rest now. I'll call again soon."

"How are things at the mine, now?" I asked. "I suppose I should say, how are the Whitneys now that the first shock is over?"

"Mrs. Whitney is holding up. She's a strong woman. But Tam"—he frowned worriedly—"I really feel he's . . . well, a bit unhinged by all this."

"I suppose losing the second son in the same tragic way would be enough to unsettle anyone," I commented quietly.

"He's always been an excitable little firebrand. When the first lad died, he made the same dramatic threats."

"Well, perhaps it was his way of releasing his unbearable grief. I suppose you just have to overlook meaningless threats in the face of such overwhelming sorrow and tragedy."

He pushed his hat back on his head, his expression thoughtful. "I'm not really all that sure they were meaningless threats," he said slowly. "A mine management man died suddenly and unexpectedly since the first Whitney boy's death."

"You aren't suggesting Tam had anything to do with the death?" I said, appalled.

He was silent for a fraction of a minute, then laughed uneasily. "Of course not. That *did* sound stupid, didn't it? Forget I said it. I suppose I'm letting my landlady, old Ma Grainey, get to me. This morning she said she wouldn't be surprised if Tam had put a curse on the mine officials. Said Bill Tyndall, Grant Roberts and myself had better watch out. That Tam Whitney's grandfather was a gypsy." He gave me a half-rueful, half-foolish smile.

I laughed, too. "No matter how enlightened we become, I suppose we all look for reasons when there are unexplained tragedies. We are all still superstitious to a degree."

He mounted his horse, then sat looking down at me. "You *will* refrain from mentioning what I've said about the death of the mine official, won't you?"

"Certainly. I've no reason to mention it to anyone," I said, shifting my sketch pads to the other arm.

"I spoke prematurely. There's certainly no evidence to link Tam with the death. But, you know, I intend to keep my eyes open. It was deemed suspicious when it hap-

pened; the man was found dead and badly battered at
the bottom of a shaft at the mine. It was assumed he'd
fallen while inspecting and that his injuries had been sustained in the fall."

I felt a sudden emptiness at the pit of my stomach as if
I'd taken an unexpected fall. There was something wrong
here in Happy Valley, I thought. Nothing that anyone
could put a finger on, but just too many little things. The
unexplained death at the mine. Mrs. Bosworth's mysterious disappearance. The cave-in. The accident, apparently
caused by a stray bullet, that had befallen me upon my arrival here. And, deny it and call it nerves as I would, my
certainty that I was being watched, followed at the quarry
this morning. Was Tam Whitney involved in all these
things? Had his sorrow at his sons' deaths unbalanced him
to the extent that he'd seek revenge on those connected
with the management of the mine? If what Richard was
implying was true, then Bill Tyndall's family might well be
in danger. And the Robertses, too. As well as Richard
Langley. But why would I be singled out to be watched or
injured? Because I was to build the Tyndalls' house? It
certainly seemed unlikely, but then, when a man was mad,
conventional reasoning was often beyond him.

"I have upset you, Minerva," Richard was saying. "I'm
sorry for that."

"Don't apologize. If there's a possibility that Tam is
. . . deranged . . . might do something violent, then it's
foolish not to think about it," I said. "Perhaps even fatal."

"At any rate, you will be careful, won't you? I can't forget that the horse was frightened by a bullet yesterday."

I smiled uneasily. "I was just thinking the same thing.
Yes, you can be certain I'll take care. Though I hope
we're upset over nothing."

He smiled reassuringly. "I'm sure that's how it will turn out to be. In the meantime, it's very nice having you in Bellefonte. I'll be calling on you soon." He turned his horse and started down Spring Street.

To my immense gratification, the Tyndalls did like the designs. I sat in a happy glow throughout the performance at the elegant new opera house, and afterward Jon and I, joined by some other young people, had a soda at the Bush House drugstore. I found it difficult to keep my mind on my companions, however, for my thoughts kept wandering back to the drawings, which I knew to be the best I'd ever done, lying on the table in the library at the Bosworth home. It was all I could do to keep from boring everyone to tears talking about my design. And my joy at finally having a chance to prove what I could do. Now, I'd show them, I thought gleefully.

And I was honest enough to admit to myself that the "them" I wanted most to show was Anthony Richmond.

I found I couldn't sleep that night. Certainly I should have been exhausted enough after the events of the past two days, but the exhilaration of getting the drawings just the way I wanted them had so excited me that I found I simply couldn't lie still. I got up quietly and lit a candle, not bothering with the gas fixtures, thinking I'd go down to the library to find something to read and, I told myself with a smile, to take one more look at the drawings. Taking up the candle and opening the door, I moved as silently as possible out into the hall. The old cherry grandfather clock in the downstairs hall struck two. There wasn't another sound in the slumbering house.

I moved silently down the stairs and into the library,

holding my candle up along the shelves until I'd found a book that appealed to me. I chose the popular *The Fair God* by Wallace. I'd promised myself I'd read it one day when I had the time. Then I turned toward the drafting table where my drawings lay. It was facing me, the drawings hidden by the slant, but even before I could see them a dreadful premonition seemed to whisper over me like a chill breeze on an otherwise warm night. I reached the table and turned it quickly toward me.

My drawings had been cut into a thousand pieces.

CHAPTER 5

A cold prickling crept along my spine as I stared in disbelief at the scattered fragments of my designs. The grandfather clock in the hall ticked like a heartbeat in the silent, watching house. I stirred uneasily and shivered, glancing nervously over my shoulder. Whoever had done this mad deed might still be nearby, watching me. I picked up my candle and moved quickly out of the library into the hall, looking into the shadows beneath the stairs.

Who would have done such a thing? Who *could* have done it? While the household slept, had one of its inhabitants crept down and cut my drawings to ribbons? Or had an outsider, knowing that the Bosworths, like most of Bellefonte's residents, never locked their doors, crept into the house and done it? Had it been Mr. Bosworth, mildly sedated as he was? Annette? Clarice, disgruntled because her Anthony had not been given the commission? Or had Anthony himself done it?

The candle flickered in a sudden draft as I went into the downstairs hall. The kitchen door stood partially ajar in the shadow cast by the stairs. The draft seemed to be coming from there. I went toward it apprehensively and pushed it open with my shoulder, shielding the candle with my hand. The back door was standing wide open. I lifted the candle to assure myself no one was still lurking in the kitchen, then crossed the room and shut the door against the damp, cold air.

As I turned around, someone was standing right over me. I gasped fearfully and drew back, holding my candle up to see the newcomer's face. It was Jon.

"Minerva. I thought I heard something down here," he said, reaching out to take my shoulders. "You're shaking. Did I startle you?"

I was indeed nearly palsied with cold and fear. "Yes. I thought for a moment you were the one who destroyed my designs," I stammered through trembling lips. "And the kitchen door was open . . ."

"Destroyed your designs?" he said unbelievingly, holding me at arm's length so he could look into my face. "Oh, no, Minerva, that can't be."

For answer, I took his hand and drew him into the library. I put my candle on the desk so he could see the ruins of my afternoon's work. He made a shocked exclamation and sifted impotently through the bits of paper.

I sank into the sofa by the fireplace. "This may be a quiet little country town, but I think there's a lot going on here," I said. "And I seem to be the target of at least part of it. Who could possibly want to do a thing like this?"

He dropped into the desk chair and stared at me across the debris on the desk. "I . . . I just don't know," he answered. "Did you say the kitchen door was ajar?"

"Yes. Someone could have come in from outside."

"Starting right now, we'll lock doors and windows at night. Although I never thought I'd see the day that would be necessary in Bellefonte."

"Well, when women disappear and mine officials die mysteriously, when shots are taken at newcomers, houses entered, and watchers lurk in the woods, I suppose it's time to take such precautions."

"Whoa, young lady. I know of all the events you mentioned except watchers in the woods. What are you talking about?"

I hesitated a moment, frowning down at my clasped hands. "I felt . . . I thought I saw someone watching me up near the quarry yesterday when we were searching for your father."

He looked worried. "Why didn't you mention it before?"

"Well, there was so much excitement when your father was found. And, to be perfectly honest, I thought I was letting my imagination run away with me. There's something about that old quarry that makes the blood run cold anyhow."

He nodded agreement. "Likely it was just another searcher like yourself. The woods were full of them yesterday."

"True, it could have been. But what about the mine official? Richard Langley mentioned there's been a mysterious death. And your mother disappearing without a trace from an area I gather she knew like the kitchen of this house. And this," I indicated the torn designs on the desk, "was a deliberate act. Someone obviously doesn't want me to build a house for your sister and brother-in-law. Oh, Jon, do you think it's possible Tam Whitney might be deranged enough by the death of his sons to do it?"

He stared at the flickering candle. "I hate to think it, but it is possible, I suppose," he said. "You'll have to be careful from now on." He touched the bits of paper. "It's a shame about this, though. The drawings were beautiful. Will you be able to replace them?"

"Yes. Certainly. They're so firmly fixed in my mind I'll have no trouble. I should think any sensible person would be aware of that, too. This little incident, I think, was in the nature of a warning."

"That sounds terribly grim."

"I know. And I can't help thinking how unlikely it would have been for Tam to know about the drawings. Or, for that matter, to have been prowling about here on the night before his son is to be buried. Yet, if he *was* prowling about and just happened to come upon the designs, his cutting them up like this seems doubly frightening and dangerous."

"Grief and a feeling of injustice—which he has good reason to feel, according to Bill—could combine to make him behave like that."

I shuddered and pulled the heavy silk rope of my dressing gown more tightly about my waist. "I'd feel a lot better if you'd search the downstairs and lock things up before we retire again," I said.

He nodded and stood up, taking the candle from the desk. He used it to light the gas fixture on the wall. "I don't imagine you'd particularly want to sit alone in the dark while I do," he said with a rueful smile.

I listened as he moved about through the downstairs rooms, locking windows and doors, my troubled thoughts mulling over everything that had happened. It *must* have been Tam Whitney, and yet I couldn't be sure. I didn't want it to be him, somehow, perhaps because I pitied him so. And, in justice, there was nothing to connect him with any of the mysterious happenings except his hatred of the mine and its officials. Almost anyone in Bellefonte *could* have been responsible, perhaps—the house being left open as it was—but who'd have a motive? I had to admit to myself that someone closer to the Tyndalls than Tam might well have done it. Someone who didn't want them to move out of this house for one reason or another. Mr. Bosworth because of his love for them? Annette because she felt she'd be breaking a promise not to leave her grandfather? Even George, perhaps, who spent his whole life trying to make Mr. Bosworth happy. I wondered briefly if Jon could have any reason to try to stop them. Had he told me the entire truth about his father's will? Or Clarice? Although I couldn't think of any reason she'd want to keep them living here, she might have been disgruntled enough by my preferment over her precious Anthony to do it.

Or, if it had been someone outside the household, who besides Tam Whitney could dislike the Tyndalls enough to want to discourage their building here? I thought of the people I'd met since arriving, Richard Langley, Mr. Roberts, and Anthony Richmond. Langley might possibly have wanted to be promoted to manager of the mine himself, I suppose, but he seemed to be Bill Tyndall's protégé. Surely, even if he were unscrupulous enough to climb on his mentor's back to success, he'd not go to such foolish lengths to discourage the building of his house. Nor did there seem to be any reason to harm an old woman. Mr. Roberts, greedy, hard-hearted boor that he was, *wanted* the Tyndalls to stay in Bellefonte.

That left Anthony Richmond. With a sinking heart, I thought he just might have considered such a macabre trick amusing. He would have known destroying the drawings wouldn't stop me, but the malicious act might have been his way of showing his contempt for my work.

But I couldn't bear to think that he'd have had anything to do with the disappearance of Mrs. Bosworth or the death at the mine.

Sighing, I shut off the gas and went out into the hall to join Jon. I was suddenly very tired. Too tired to puzzle over it any more tonight. One thing was certain, though. From now on, my drawings would be locked up when I was away from the house. And I would be watchful of everyone.

I stepped out into the darkened front hall and paused at the foot of the steps, waiting for Jon to complete his inspection of the cellars and first floor rooms. A sudden light tapping at the inner set of front doors caused me to start violently. Heart racing, I took a step toward the kitchen door to call Jon, not wanting to awaken the family by doing so from where I stood. Then, thinking it was singularly cowardly of me to require Jon's presence to confront the unknown caller, I turned back toward the door. After all, I reasoned, if whoever was there meant me any harm, he'd certainly not tap politely to be let in. Moreover, one loud scream from me would bring help quickly to my side.

I paused at the marble-topped table near the front door and lit another of the candles that were kept there. The door opened as the late caller saw the flash of the match. As I turned to face him, the flickering candle revealed Anthony Richmond casually and quietly shutting the door behind him.

"I noticed a light in the library as I passed. Is anything wrong?" he asked, his habitual faint smile looking somehow malicious in the soft light.

"You were passing at this hour?" I whispered, acutely

aware of my untidy hair and robe as I had not been with Jon.

"I was working late at the house on Linn Street," he explained.

"Working at two o'clock in the morning?" I said, my voice rising a little in disbelief.

He stared at me coolly. "I often do. Does that bother you?"

"Not in the least. But having *my* work destroyed does," I retorted. "And it's mighty coincidental, your being in the neighborhood just when it happened."

He shut his lips on his enigmatic smile and shook his head as if in exasperation. Then, taking my arm, he urged me toward the small parlor to the right of the front door. "No need to wake the family," he said in an explanatory way as he shut the double doors behind us.

He turned to face me, crossing his arms judiciously on his chest. "Now would you mind explaining to me just what it is you're babbling about. What is all this about your work being destroyed?"

"Don't you know?" I said spitefully. "Really, a childish act of vandalism and one that will cost me no more than two hours' work. I'm surprised you'd stoop to it."

"Stoop to *what?*" he said with exaggerated patience as though speaking to a scatter-brained child.

"I'll show you what I mean," I snapped, taking his hand and leading him to the library door at the rear of the parlor, the candle in my other hand held up dramatically to point the way. We passed through the doorway, and I stepped aside to let him move ahead to where the drafting table lay in full view, the scattered bits of paper a crazy collage across its surface. "There," I said bitterly, "as if you didn't know."

He stepped up to the table and sifted the pieces through his fingers much as Jon had done. His face was turned slightly from me so that I couldn't read his expression. Suddenly, I wanted to see the expression in the luminous dark eyes. More than anything on earth, I hoped they'd register horror as Jon's had done when he looked at the destruction of my sketches. That would surely mean that he'd had nothing to do with it. I moved up beside him, holding the candle to illuminate his face, but when he turned to meet my eyes, I could read no expression whatsoever.

"Whoever did it certainly made a thorough job of it," he commented.

"Yes," I said dryly.

"And you think I did it?"

"You certainly could have. You walked right into the house before I could really answer the door tonight. You are well aware it's never locked."

"And because I'm familiar with the Bosworths' habits, *I* did it. Thank you very much for your good opinion of me," was the sarcastic reply.

"Oh, you're quite welcome," I said, undaunted. "Your familiarity with the house was only incidental, however. Half the town shares that knowledge. There are other reasons you would do this."

"Oh, I understand," he said mockingly. "Because I didn't fall into mindless ecstasies over your sacred designs yesterday you think I destroyed them."

He was making me sound like an egocentric hothead, I realized angrily, and even more angrily, I knew that I was acting like one. "Well, you *did* resent my being given the commission to build the Tyndalls' new house," I said more moderately.

He laughed shortly. "You really must get rid of those feelings of persecution," he said. "I have more commissions just now than I can handle."

I imagined that might be true. He was the only architect in town and, moreover, was highly regarded. Bellefonte was a thriving little community with much building going on. I bit my lip awkwardly. Could it be that I was jealous of his seemingly easy success?

He smiled as if reading some of what I was thinking. Then, with a thoughtful look at the bits of paper on the drafting table, he cleared his throat. "Will you have any trouble getting your ideas down on paper again?" he asked kindly.

"No. I find that once I have the concept firmly in mind, I can do a second version without even consulting my first sketches. Often it's much better."

He nodded in agreement. "That's exactly how it is with me. Look, I'm sorry this happened. If there's any way I can help you, if you need any materials, please let me know."

I gazed at him wonderingly. He was really *nice*, I thought in surprise. When he wasn't showing off his gallantry for a featherhead like Clarice or trying to put me, a pushy female, in her place, he was honest and kind.

"Thank you," I said humbly. "I . . . I . . . shouldn't have made such a wild accusation. It was so upsetting to come down here and find this had happened."

"I'm sure it was," he said soberly. "And while there have been some incidents that make this seem sinister—like the way Tam burst out against Bill at the mine yesterday—I think it's more than likely that you have to look no further than little Annette for the answer to this mystery."

"Do you really think she would have done this?"

"It can't have escaped you that she'd like nothing better than to stay here in her grandfather's house," he said complacently.

I thought of the conversation I'd had with Annette the day I arrived. Doubtless he was right. Here I was building a series of accidents into a mysterious conspiracy when, likely as not, it was merely a small girl's protest against moving. I smiled at my own foolishness.

"You're very pretty when you smile," he said almost shyly.

That was the last thing in the world I expected from him. I was utterly disarmed and felt myself blushing. "Thank you," I stammered, feeling the candle wavering in my hand. I glanced up at him quickly and there was admiration in his eyes. A tiny muscle twitched in his cheek and he wavered closer to me. Then, suddenly, his smile was mocking again.

"How gratifying to know you *are* a woman under that businesslike exterior. You react to a compliment like any other female."

"Of course," I said a bit stiffly, feeling rebuffed somehow.

"Now you're all starch and choler again," he teased. "Like Susan B. Anthony. A man-hater. But she's old and sour and ugly, so a person can understand her reacting like that . . ."

"She wasn't always old and sour and ugly," I flared. "She got that way after years of beating her head against a stone wall. She has spent her entire life trying to get conceited men to realize that women have minds as good as men, and they're every bit as concerned with who governs the country. The abuse she's taken would be enough to make anyone sour and old."

He threw up his hands as if in exasperation. "This is what comes of trying to pay you a compliment," he said in an affronted way.

"All your compliments are smug and superior, just like you are," I snapped. "Unless one happens to be a syrupy little belle like Clarice, whose entire life is spent waiting to be told how feminine and graceful and lovely she is."

"And you don't like to be told you're feminine and graceful and lovely?" he added, maddeningly.

"I'd rather have one sincere compliment about my contribution to the world than all those false ones you give Clarice that are calculated to keep her sweet and docile and no threat to your feelings of masculine superiority."

"Nevertheless, I think you'd like to have some of them, too. Why don't you behave in a way to make men want to give you courtly compliments?"

"Oh, *damn* your compliments!" I seethed. "I don't need them and I don't want them."

I heard Jon finishing his inspection and locking up in the front hall. With an effort, I tried to calm down and banish the angry lines from my face. In a moment, he'd walked back down the hall and opened the library door.

"I heard the Fire Company bell just now, Minerva," he said as he opened the door. "I'm afraid it's down at the bottom of the hill on Allegheny Street. That's the fourth since May . . ." Then, catching sight of Anthony Richmond, "Hello, Tony, where did you drop from?"

"I was just explaining to Minerva that I was working late at the house on Linn Street when I saw the lights here. I stopped to see if something was wrong."

"Did you notice the fire when you came down Linn?" Jon said.

"No. No, I can't say that I did," was the reply.

"It must have gone fast, then. I can see the flames now."

"Perhaps we'd better go see if there's anything we can do," I suggested.

"No, we'd only be in the way. Besides, as a doctor, I think you've had quite enough excitement in the last few days. Did you tell Anthony about your drawings?"

"Yes," I said shortly, wishing the obnoxious Tony would make a move to leave.

"Minerva thinks perhaps Tam Whitney might have come into the house and done it," Jon continued.

"Is *that* what Minerva thinks?" Anthony said in amusement.

"Anthony seems to think perhaps Annette did it—not wanting to move away," I interjected hastily.

Jon laughed lightly. "I'd hate to think the little minx could do such a thing, but I must confess, I hope that's what it proves to be, and that all those other mysterious happenings have no connection."

"What other mysterious happenings?" Anthony said.

"Oh, the death at the mine. Mother's disappearance. The shot at Duchess. Someone watching Minerva up at the quarry. And, come to think of it, these fires lately."

Anthony burst out laughing. "In short, every accident or calamity in Bellefonte for the last year. Really, our Minerva has a lively feminine imagination, Jon, but I can't imagine you abetting her."

"I think perhaps we should break up this discussion until another time," I said, gritting my teeth. "We're going to wake the entire household."

Anthony bowed politely, his black eyes still amused, and led the way to the front door. Jon stepped forward and unlocked the door to let him out. "Really, Tony, you work too hard if you're still at it at two o'clock in the morning," he said conversationally. "No one but a doctor should be up at such an ungodly hour."

"The price of being a good architect, my friend," he said smugly. "I can't keep up with the demand for my services." He threw me a look which seemed to mock me. "Any good architect would tell you the same thing," he added with a decided emphasis on the adjective.

My temper flared scarlet. "With half the town burning down, no doubt you're right," I snapped. "I wouldn't put it past you to set the fires yourself to drum up business."

His face turned pale in the flickering candlelight. "I don't find that amusing at all," he said icily. Then, jamming his hat on his head, he murmured a hasty good-bye to Jon and went out, shutting the door firmly behind him. In a moment, the outer door opened and closed and he was gone into the blackness beyond.

"Well," I said with satisfaction although I felt strangely regretful, "I never thought I'd be able to take the wind out of Mr. Anthony Richmond's sails."

Jon stared after him. "He's not as conceited as he sometimes sounds, Minerva," he said, with gentle chiding, "and lately, the town wags, you know, the old fellows who sit on the bench outside the courthouse, have been teasing him a bit roughly about that very thing. They tell him his business has never been so good. That maybe he's starting the fires himself. It's become a town joke."

"Oh, I didn't know that," I said, feeling stupid and cruel. I hadn't really set out to hurt him, after all, I'd wanted only to say something utterly outrageous to pay

him back for his ill-concealed contempt of my abilities.
I'd wanted to slap him down a bit, draw a little blood in
combat. Well, I'd surely done that all right. And I didn't
like myself a bit for it. "I didn't know," I repeated.

"Of course you didn't. He'll understand that when he's
cooled off. Don't worry about it. You look exhausted, Minerva. You must get back to bed. We'll do what we can in
the morning to get to the bottom of this."

I nodded bleakly and followed him up the stairs, trying
to forget the stricken look on Anthony's face. I wished
passionately that I'd never made the ugly remark and that
he'd realize I hadn't known about the town joke—that I
wasn't a vicious woman, just a very angry one.

But try as I would to ignore it, I had to admit to myself
that I was feeling a very definite physical and emotional
attraction to the man in spite of the fury he aroused in
me. What kind of fool was I to allow such a thing to happen to me? He was the very epitome of the kind of man I
could most do without. The only thing he liked about
women was their softness and "femininity." Honesty,
brains and self-reliance, the qualities I most prided myself
on, were something I ought to be ashamed to admit to in
his opinion. Why could he not see that they were *human*
qualities to be admired, not only for men but for women
and children, too? I was suddenly furious at myself for
losing my temper and saying something to him which
forced me to feel shame and compassion afterward. What
I wanted most in the world to do at this time was to hate
him.

And he certainly gave me reason. He mocked and insulted me. In an attempt to discourage me from staying in
Bellefonte, perhaps he'd even cut up my drawings thinking Annette would be blamed. For silly as the idea might

seem, he *had* been in the neighborhood in the middle of the night.

Just how much was Anthony Richmond prepared to do to protect his territory from an interloper?

In the morning, Jon told the family what had happened to my drawings and the Tyndalls, shocked and subdued, agreed that the house should be kept locked from then on and the library as well when I wasn't working there.

Bill Tyndall seemed older than his years this morning, his usual cheerful smile forced and distant. When he and Annette had left the house for work and school respectively, Alice confided that he'd slept badly, fretting over Tam Whitney's obvious hatred and the fact that he would have liked to attend the funeral service for the dead boy but feared his presence would bring pain to the parents, perhaps even precipitate another scene. So he'd gone to work as usual, fearing the other miners would consider him insensible.

Alice left the house later in the morning, saying she was taking a baked ham and some other food to the Whitneys' neighbor for anonymous giving to the bereaved family after the services. I could see that the miner's death had affected both her and her husband deeply. I hoped that Tam would come to see that the Nittany mine's new manager was the best thing that had ever happened to the coal-mining region. How much good Bill Tyndall could do if given a chance.

I worked most of the morning and completed the drawings with even better detail than the ones that had been destroyed. I locked them in the library and went in search of George to beg a cup of tea.

He quickly set it steeping and produced a plate of cookies to go with it.

"Where is everyone, George?" I said, flexing my back and accepting the cup he offered me.

"The ol' mister is still sleeping. Miss Clarice, too. Mr. Jon gone on calls. Mary's gone to market."

"She's a quiet little thing, George," I said, "I've hardly seen her since I arrived. Just a glimpse of a neat, quick little woman sweeping through the house with linens or cleaning supplies."

He chuckled and poured me more tea. "She's a busy little somebody all right," he said fondly. "A lot younger than me, too. I reckon I'm a mighty lucky man, finding the Bosworths and her, too, here in the north. Would you like to see the secret room now, miss? I got a few minutes before I start dinner if you'd care to see it."

"Oh, I'd love to. I'd forgotten about it in the excitement of the last two days."

"Well, then, come along," he said delightedly.

He led the way up the back stairs which mounted in a series of sharp turns clear to the third floor. At the top of the attic stairs stood a small closet. To the right of it was a further flight of narrow stairs leading to the widow's walk, which I considered an anachronism in this inland town.

George opened the door of the closet which was filled with old dresses and coats. He swept them aside with one hand and pulled on what seemed to be an old leather belt lying on the floor. A large section of the plank floor lifted up, revealing a dark hole from which the top of a ladder showed.

He grinned in satisfaction at my open-mouthed appreciation. I stepped back and ran my eye over the wall area facing the third-floor stairs. The room was concealed in what appeared to be just the rather low ceiling over the stairs. It was actually built between the second and third floors.

George fished a candle and matches from his pocket and lit them, stepping gingerly onto the ladder.

"It's fastened tight to the wall, but you be careful when you follow me down," he cautioned. "Jest wait till I light the candle down there."

I watched as he descended into the black void, the flickering candle making fantastic shadows on the ladder. In a moment, he called from below for me to come.

I did so, holding my skirts to prevent tripping over them. It was not an easy descent for the rungs were better than a foot apart and, perpendicular with the wall, left little toe room. When I reached the floor, I found I was in a six-foot-square cubicle containing only a rough wooden bedstead covered with a faded quilt and a minuscule table upon which stood a cracked glass candleholder. It was eerie and dusty with only the light from the two candles; the clothes in the closet above effectively screened out any light from the gloomy attic.

"No one would ever detect this room," I said in amazement. "But how on earth could a person stand it? I think more than an hour in this place and I'd be raving."

George's face took on a strained look. "It ain't exzacly fun, miss, but I stayed in worse till I got here. It was worth it."

I shuddered and started climbing back up. I didn't like the little room which was not much bigger than a grave. George clambered after me, first snuffing the candle on the little table.

"What about air, George?" I asked as he dropped the trap door back into place.

"If there was no immediate danger, the Bosworths jest left this door open. Even with the clothes hanging over it, that gave enough air. But if there was slave finders in the neighborhood, it was put down. Then there was enough air to last p'raps twenty minutes if a person kept still."

"I should go mad."

He shook his head reminiscently. "It wasn't easy. But soon's the men that was looking for me moved on, the Bosworths had me carried downstairs to the room you're staying in now. They nursed me with their own hands," he added proudly.

"They seem to be fine people," I said. "I can understand why you didn't want to leave here."

"They the best people the Lord ever made, miss," he said, snuffing the candle and putting it back in his pocket. "Though ol' Mister and ol' Missus sure did a heap of fightin' between them."

"They did?" I said, remembering that Annette had also remarked about her grandparents fussing at one another. "But he seems to have been so devoted to her. So anxious about her."

"I didn't *say* he wasn't devoted to her. Nor her to him, neither. But, Lordy, could them two *fight!* Once I seen ol' Mister up-dump a pitcher of water on her head."

I laughed in spite of myself. The picture of dignified and handsome old Mr. Bosworth so losing control of himself was ludicrous.

"What did she say to that?"

"Picked up the bread dough Mary had raisin' on the shelf above the stove and pushed it into his face," he said complacently. "Oh, things was never dull around here for one minute. They kept things goin' all the time."

"What on earth did they fight about?" I said wonderingly.

He laughed reminiscently. "Anythin'. Everythin'. Them two, they was like birds that shouldn't never have shared the same nest. They was both as good as the live-longest day, but there was no way they'd look at the world the same way. Ol' Missus, she loved the mountains and the streams. She had an ol' fishin' rod and come a nice day, you'd find her down by Spring Creek with the little boys who'd played hooky from school. She was a teensy little ol' lady, pretty as a violet in spring, but she knew more about these hills and woods than the men who hire themselves out to city folk for guides. While ol' Mister, he like books and reading and painting pictures. He worry all the time that she step on a copperhead or fall down a bank and break her leg. She jest laugh at him. He'd say she jest roamed the woods to agg'avate him, and she say he try to stop her and make her turn into a little ol' prissy lady doing needlepoint so she can't have no fun. They was a pair, all right. Um-*um!*"

"I certainly wouldn't have suspected they fought so much from the way he's been so broken up over her disappearance," I said as we reached the second floor.

"Like I tol' you. Way they fussed don't mean anythin'. They'd have died for each other, but they fight worse than the Yankee and Johnny Reb boys."

We went on down to the kitchen. Mary had come back and was paring potatoes at the sink. She threw me a shy smile. "Miss Alice is home and wants to see you when you got time, miss," she said. "She's in the parlor."

I thanked her and her husband, too, for the tour of the

slave room, then went into the hallway to the parlor. I checked the library door to be sure it was locked, almost compulsively as I passed it, thinking of what George had said about old Mr. and Mrs. Bosworth being almost constant combatants. George seemed entirely positive of their mutual devotion in spite of their incompatibility. I wondered suddenly if "Ol' Mister" could have gotten angry enough with her to have killed her but immediately thrust the thought away as shameful. He'd been asleep in his room when she disappeared anyhow.

Or so it had seemed.

My work on the house plans proceeded beautifully. With Alice's enthusiastic approval, I completed them, the specifications, and even visited the local lumberyard to place orders for the materials we'd need. It was too late in the season to break ground for winter had arrived even earlier than usual in central Pennsylvania. By the second week in December, I had done all I could until spring. Accordingly, I told the family at breakfast one morning that I was going to the train station to arrange for my trip back to Philadelphia, and would return when the weather broke in the spring.

"You can't go, Minerva," Annette cried. "There's to be a pageant at school next week and I specifically promised everyone you'd be there. My friends want to see you."

"Oh, but darling, I can't stay. My work is done until the ground thaws in the spring."

"Why can't you stay?" Alice said. Then, with a wicked grin, "I know your clients are likely banging down your door, Minerva, but, like us, they can't break ground till spring. Why can't you stay the winter with us?"

I smiled at her teasing reference to my clients, non-

existent except for the Tyndalls. But they would be banging down my door if the design won the *American Architect and Builder* contest. With the Tyndalls' permission, I
had entered it.

"Really, I would feel like the man who came to dinner
and stayed forty years until he died."

"Suppose you undertake to add a porch . . . a sun
porch really, on the side of this house, Minerva," Mr. Bosworth said suddenly.

"Oh, sir, I think you're just being kind," I said hur-
riedly.

"Indeed, I am not. I love this old house far too much to
suggest you build something onto it just to be 'kind,'" the
old gentleman assured me. "Jenny always says that old
porch is useless as it is, exposed to the sun all morning
and afternoon. She wants it glass-enclosed so she can
keep flowers there. Even, perhaps, enjoy the sun a bit on
winter days. I've studied the design for Bill and Alice's
house with much interest. I'm convinced you could do
justice to what I want. And it could be done in the winter
all right. Once the framing and windows were in, the
work would be all under roof."

"Are you quite certain you really want it?" I said, putting down my napkin.

"Of course. Or I would not have made the offer," he
said with a smile.

"All right. I'll do it," I said.

Annette jumped up and ran around the table to hug
me. "Oh, I'm so glad," she said. "You'll be with us for
Christmas and the New Year's Eve Masquerade Ball at
the Bush Arcade. Oh, Minerva, I'm so glad you're here.
This winter will be such fun."

I caught her to me and smiled into her bright eyes.

"Even though I'm designing a house that will take you out of Grandad's home?"

She smiled awkwardly. "He's getting used to the idea," she said, reaching out to take her grandfather's hand. "And he says my room will always be here in case I want to stay with him sometimes when Dad and Mother have to go away."

"I'm glad, Annette," I said.

"Then it's settled," Bill Tyndall said as he wiped his mouth and stood up. "You see, Minerva, we've all become fond of you. You're like one of the family. I think, perhaps, you'd best design one of those rooms in our house exactly the way you want it. We'll expect you to visit often."

Alice stood too, and proffered her cheek for his good-bye kiss.

"You've made the whole family happy by agreeing, Minerva," she said warmly.

But later, when Clarice arose, I wasn't so certain.

She sought me out in the library where I was hunting a sketch pad to make some preliminary drawings of the proposed porch.

"George says you're staying on for the winter," she said noncommittally. "That you're going to enclose the side porch for Father."

"Yes. I'm honored that he wants me to."

She sat down on the couch by the fireplace, lounging back with a nonchalance that put me instantly on the defensive. Her smile was without warmth.

"It's a shame you don't confine your practice to Philadelphia leaving little old Bellefonte to a local man," she said sweetly with a slight emphasis on the last word.

"You mean Anthony Richmond, of course," I replied levelly. "But it seems he already has more business than he can conveniently handle. I understand he has actually been turning down commissions. At any rate, I'll be leaving Bellefonte when your sister and brother-in-law's house is completed and will certainly be no threat to him."

I stared at her a little defiantly. Try as I might, I couldn't truly like her, although she'd become increasingly pleasant to me during my stay in Bellefonte. Providing Anthony Richmond wasn't around. When he was, she became coquettish, slightly catty and consistently antagonistic toward me, treating my being an architect as a very bad joke. It was as if she was certain no *woman* could possibly succeed in the profession *he*, a great big, clever man had chosen to grace. I thought her behavior false and affected when Anthony or, indeed, any of her male admirers was around and wondered why she didn't just act herself. When she wasn't trying to impress some man, she was really a fairly nice person.

And I was honest enough to admit to myself that I didn't like her because *she* appeared to have Anthony in the curve of her little palm.

"I never thought you *would* be a threat to him," she replied, as if the idea was highly amusing. "And, as you point out, he certainly doesn't need the work. I'm sure Father and Bill and Alice are happy to give you a chance."

Her tone implied that only charity prompted their generosity to an inferior craftsman. I gritted my teeth and said nothing. After all, she was the daughter of the house, and if she chose to be patronizing with me, it was to her shame, not mine.

She got up and sauntered over to the library window,

pulling the drape aside to look out at the snow that was beginning to spit sporadically from the leaden skies. I concentrated on sharpening my pencils, trying to ignore the elegant back turned toward me. After a long moment, she turned toward me, staring haughtily down her slender nose as if amused at my inept attempts to ignore her.

"Just be careful, my dear Minerva, that you do not outstay your welcome in Bellefonte," she said at last. "We do not like outsiders here."

Without waiting for me to reply, she swept from the library, leaving me to stare open-mouthed at the closing door.

There had been no mistaking the note of dislike in the silken, too-sweet voice. And her statement had sounded decidedly like a threat.

CHAPTER 6

The weeks before Christmas were full with work progressing on the sun porch, programs at Annette's school and church, and parties all over Bellefonte. We were all invited to a holiday tea at the neighboring mansion of Governor Beaver. It was an impressive three story structure with a mansard roof on the corner of Allegheny and Curtin streets just above the Bosworth house. I passed it whenever I visited the Tyndall house site, and Clarice had once remarked that Anthony Richmond had assisted in its design. If she'd meant to impress me with that information, she'd succeeded for the house was truly magnificent.

Bellefonte was proud of Governor Beaver and ex-Governor Andrew Gregg Curtin who'd governed the Commonwealth during the Civil War. Both men had been the first choice for Vice-Presidential candidates; Curtin was Ulysses S. Grant's first choice and Beaver was Garfield's. Neither man had accepted the nomination, however. Years before, there'd been another governor of Pennsylvania from Bellefonte, William Bigler, and Mr. Bosworth's favorite gentle joke was that the water from Talleyrand's fountain produced greatness in the town's citizens. Governor Curtin was a guest today, making a rare excursion outside his home for he was frail and ill. He'd been installed in a comfortable chair beside the fire, a plaid robe across his lap and the guests crowded around him, wishing him well and offering him their affection. I could see why he was so beloved with his pale, gentle face and large eyes. He must have been wearied by the attention, but he seemed happy to speak to each well-wisher.

I sat quietly on a "lady's" chair, sipping a cup of unwanted tea and trying to keep a tiny plate of cookies from slipping off my lap. Although I was delighted to have been included in the Bosworth family's invitation to tea, the occasion had proved to be considerably more elegant than I'd anticipated and I felt out of place in my plain tweed skirt and ruffled blouse. Moreover, the family had temporarily abandoned me, and I didn't see anyone I knew well enough to engage in conversation. So I was smiling stiffly in what I hoped was a friendly manner and trying not to think everyone was looking at me, which in fact, they were not, when someone spoke at my elbow.

"You look about as uncomfortable as I am in this gathering, young lady. I can understand why *you* were invited, but why an old Democrat like me should be included in this Republican shindig, I don't understand."

I looked up to meet the twinkling eyes of Mr. P. Gray Meek, the editor of the *Democratic Watchman*.

"Oh, Mr. Meek, I think politics are forgotten and rightly so during the Christmas time, don't you?" I said.

He laughed and pulled up a chair to sit down beside me. "I suppose you're right. But a few years back, some of these Republicans were accusing me of stealing everything, even a red-hot stove, unless it was nailed down. Though where they got the idea the Almighty intended the rich to 'own' the good things of the world, I don't know." He looked around the room cynically. "This house is full of ironmasters, coal-mine owners and politicians," he remarked, "but it's the ordinary people who dig the coal and smelt the iron who make them rich. I'll continue to say so as long as I live."

"I'm sure they must respect your right to do so or you'd not be here," I pointed out.

"Oh, but if I weren't, who'd report this gala occasion in the paper?"

I laughed at the comical expression on his alert little face. "Oh, Mr. Meek, I don't think they care about that. Bellefonte has more newspapers than grocery stores. If you didn't report the party, the others would." I sipped at my rapidly cooling tea. "Besides, all the ironmasters and coal-mine owners and officials aren't rapacious. I'm developing quite an admiration for Bill Tyndall and his policies. He says someday machines will do the exceptionally dangerous work presently being done by men in the coal mines."

He nodded brusquely. "Bill Tyndall's a sound man," he agreed. "He really cares about the people who work under him, I think. And I've no doubt his views about getting machines to do the dangerous work are held with only the most humanitarian motives. But I have a very healthy apprehension about machines taking work from men, whatever the reason. It could be the most debilitating trend this country ever saw."

I had to smile at the notion of machines ever becoming a threat to men's welfare. Mr. Meek was a likable little man for all his unpolished edges, but he certainly held unorthodox ideas.

"Well, I understand there have been too many deaths in the mines here, and if machines are to be used, I hope they will relieve *that* problem."

He frowned and thrust his hands into his waistcoat pockets. "I'm afraid at least one of those deaths would have occurred no matter how many machines were employed. I was there when the sheriff investigated the death of Jason Peters. I *still* can't imagine why a mine official would be inspecting without a helmet . . . and wearing a Sunday suit. Nor how he got so battered just falling down a shaft."

I remembered Richard Langley mentioning the death as being mysterious. And bearing, as it seemed to, on the other suspicious happenings in the town over the past months, it piqued my curiosity. "Do you, then, believe the man was murdered?" I said bluntly.

He cocked an amused eye at me. "I'm a newspaper man and am careful how I word things," he said, grinning. "In my newspaper, I just noted the unexpected death of an official of the Nittany Coal Company."

"But you were not satisfied with the accidental verdict?"

"Of course not."

"Mr. Meek, can I ask what you thought of Mrs. Bosworth's disappearance?" I said softly.

His mobile face rapidly turned inquisitive. "You aren't trying to suggest the two events were connected, are you?"

I fiddled with my teaspoon, wishing I hadn't mentioned it in just that way. Without the incidents that had involved me, I certainly would not have thought there was any connection. And I had no intention of telling the little editor of my tribulations. To him, all information was grist for his newspaper mill. "Oh, not really," I stammered. "It's just that both the death and the disappearance were somewhat peculiar. I understand Mrs. Bosworth was quite at home in the woods. It seems odd that she has completely disappeared. I mean, I could understand if she met with an accident. A fall or snake bite or even drowning in the quarry, but then, wouldn't her body have been recovered?"

"It's one of those mysteries that will never be answered, I suppose," he said. "Like the Bosworths themselves. Hard to understand."

"I really don't know why you'd say that," I protested. "I think they're a remarkably open family."

"Oh, I dare say." He shook his head and frowned as if trying to pinpoint what he meant. "They're fine people and Jonathon Bosworth is an old and dear friend of mine. But I never understood them all the same. If I fought with a woman as bad as he did with his wife, I wouldn't live with her. What's more, I can't understand Jenny Bosworth staying either. Yet, and you may quote me on it, I never knew a couple who loved each other more dearly. Makes you realize more than ever that hate is the reverse side of love. Like a coin. Inseparable. The potential for great love and great hate are in every relationship between a man and woman."

I thought of Anthony Richmond and nodded agreement.

"The children seem to have loved her very much, too," I observed. "And little Annette."

"Yes. Though Jon was her favorite. Still, the girls were the ones Jonathon favored, so it seemed to balance out. But the sibling rivalry in that family when they were little was enough to make their parents' feuding seem nothing." He shook his head and laughed reminiscently. "Pugnacious little children. Probably because they were Irish."

"They seem to get along well enough now," I said,

wondering for the first time if old sibling resentments still stirred under the Bosworth children's calm exteriors. "I think they're a very affectionate family."

"Don't pay any attention to me. I'm just an incurable old gossip. Failing of newspaper men." He leaned over and patted my hand. "Anyway, I didn't come over here to chat about the Bosworths. Nor Bellefonte's industries and politics. I want to know how the plans for Minerva's Citadel are coming along."

I stared at him in bafflement. "Minerva's Citadel? Wherever did you get such a name for the house?"

"That's what Anthony Richmond called it last time I talked to him about the one he's building on Allegheny Street. He says it's like a woman's idea of a castle."

"Oh, blast that man," I snapped angrily, then lifted my handkerchief to hide my outburst. "I wish he'd choke on his own supercilious smile."

He threw back his head and laughed. "Anthony's not a bad sort. Sometimes what he says seems to come out with a more superior, authoritative sound than he means it to. He's an extremely intelligent and well-informed man. I suppose that's why."

"He's also very prejudiced. If something is innovative and different, he scoffs at it. And I deeply resent his assumption that a woman can't compare with a man in a given profession."

He leaned close and whispered conspiratorially. "Don't be so sure of that. Perhaps it's because they're secretly convinced that women *can*, that so many men profess to believe in male superiority. Anthony's not alone in that. But when the right woman comes along, she'll tame the savage beast."

I stared then at the young man in question who was

dutifully accepting a dainty bit of cookie from Clarice's charmingly held fingers, his mouth open like a rather stupid fish. *I* wouldn't feed him like a pet lapdog to show my power over him, I thought resentfully. I'd treat him with respect and dignity, as I expected him to treat me. Mr. Meek's eyes followed mine and he smiled ironically.

"Perhaps she's already started," he said.

I had been working on the sun porch steadily. Yet, I knew my small income wouldn't cover great expenditures. For these reasons, I hadn't completed my Christmas shopping. So, a few days before Christmas, I suspended work on the plans for the porch to visit Bellefonte's small business section. There I purchased a small present, inexpensive but chosen with thought and care, for everyone in the family, including George, Mary and Louise, the "day" girl, and was walking back up Allegheny Street when I met Mrs. Grant Roberts. She was walking along jerkily, her pinched little face blue with cold in spite of the fine furs she wore. When she caught sight of me, she stopped me with a nervous outstretched hand.

"Oh, Miss Stewart. I'm so happy to run into you like this," she said softly, dabbing at her blue little nose. "I've so been wanting an opportunity to apologize for our rudeness the night you came to Bellefonte. It was unforgivable, embarrassing you as we did . . ."

"You weren't in the least rude, Mrs. Roberts," I said truthfully. It was her *husband* who had been.

"It's kind of you to say so, but I still feel badly." She seemed to take notice of the packages in my arms. "I see you've been shopping. I'm just on my way. Grant finally consented to let me buy our hired girl a Christmas present provided I don't spend more than a dollar." She sighed perceptibly. "I wonder, would you walk along with me and give me some advice?" she asked wistfully. "I so seldom get a chance to talk with anyone."

I hesitated. The packages were unwieldy and I was tired, but poor little Mrs. Roberts looked as though it was truly important to her to have me agree. Her loneliness was an almost palpable thing.

"Of course. If you'll let me buy you an ice cream soda at the drugstore first. I'd like an opportunity to put these things down for a while."

"Oh, let's leave them in my front hall. You can pick them up on your way back," she said, turning back to her house which was only a few steps away.

We left the packages in the care of her hired girl and started back to the center of town. Upon reaching Brown's drugstore, we took a back table and ordered chocolate sodas. When they were served, Mrs. Roberts sipped hers almost ecstatically. "This is so nice," she observed. "I so seldom get out of the house. There's always so much work to do. And Grant discourages me making friends here in Bellefonte."

I stared at her unbelievingly. "Why on earth would he do that?"

She sighed and her pretty green eyes took on a slightly glassy look. "He *says* because he doesn't like the town, and we'll be leaving soon. As soon as Bill Tyndall satisfies my husband. But I know it's because he just doesn't like me having friends. Says it gives me modern ideas."

I laughed uncomfortably. She was so candid and yet so pathetic. It must have been terribly hard for her, married to the brutalizing Roberts. And she seemed to have no defenses against his bullying.

"I don't think friends ever do a person any harm," I

said. "Perhaps you ought to brave your husband's disapproval to have some."

"I would like to make a friend of you . . . and of Alice Tyndall," she said, still in the little-girl wistful voice. "I do admire courageous women so much."

I laughed at that. "I've never thought of myself as courageous. Nor do I suppose Alice considers herself so."

"Oh, but she is. You are. I'd never have the courage to learn a profession. Or speak out on things the way you both do." Her face took on an expression at once secret and yearning. "Indeed, I am quite jealous of you both. Sometimes I almost hate you."

"That hardly seems fair," I said with a smile. "We both worked hard to learn our professions. Nobody waved a magic wand to give us our knowledge. Besides, I'm sure in a million years, I could never manage that big house and the children as you do with practically no help. Perhaps your accomplishments outrank mine."

"Don't patronize me," she hissed, suddenly and totally hostile. "I *know* you women who had a chance to be something besides constant mothers hate and laugh at women like me."

"Oh, no, Mrs. Roberts. Of course I don't feel like that. Nor, I can assure you, does Alice. She's the most loving and generous of women . . ."

But her eyes were glinting with a strange, slightly mad anger. She flexed her hands convulsively on the marble tabletop, staring at me fixedly. Then, suddenly, she swept her arm out and dashed the chocolate soda to the floor. The other patrons stared open-mouthed as she jumped to her feet, upsetting the small wire chair. "I . . . I don't want to shop after all," she cried. "And Grant may come

home. He'll be angry to find me gone so long. I'll leave
your packages on the front porch. Good day."

With that she swept from the little drugstore, leaving
me staring in amazement at her retreating back.

She had seemed quite insane for a moment, I thought.
Insane enough to have destroyed my sketches, or worse?

On Christmas Eve, Jon asked me to take a walk with
him through the freshly fallen snow before the guests arrived for the company supper that had been planned.

"Oh, that sounds lovely. I'll call Annette," I said.

"No. Not this time," he said quickly. "Just you and me.
I want to talk to you privately."

Mystified by his words, I donned boots, cloak and hat.
We let ourselves out and Jon took my arm, steering me up
Curtin Street toward the house site.

We walked along, past the Beaver mansion and the few
other houses and were finally on the snow-covered wagon
track. Every tree and twig was outlined with white on
top. Indeed, the whole world was a panorama of black
and white and varying shades of deep, deep green in the
hemlocks and firs. Snow was still falling gently, but occa-
sionally, a shaft of sunlight would break through the
heavy cloud cover turning the snow on the distant mountains to salmon-pink beneath the denuded trees. When
we reached the house site, the view of the mountains
through the gap was more subdued than it had been in
October but just as breathtaking. I could hardly wait to
start building.

We paused and I smiled at Jon. "What is it that you
were so anxious to talk to me about? So far, we've
discussed the fact that the mountain roads are drifted
shut and that it's expected to be very cold tonight and

that it's nice to have snow for Christmas, but none of those subjects seem of such importance that we should have excluded Annette from our walk."

He took my hands and turned me to face him. Snow was beginning to settle on his blond eyelashes, making his gray eyes silvery in the fading light. I could not read the expression in them as he stared down at me with a whimsical smile.

"Haven't you guessed, Minerva?" he said softly. "Haven't you noticed how much I care for you?"

I lowered my eyes from his fond and probing stare. Had I realized he was becoming attracted to me? I thought that yes, in all honesty, I had been slightly aware of it.

He lifted my chin with one gloved finger. "Forgive me, Minerva. How ungallant of me to assume you were aware of it and to try to force you to acknowledge it. What I meant to say . . . what I brought you here to say is that I've come to love you deeply since you've entered my life. I was so glad my sister persuaded you to stay with us until spring for if she hadn't, I swear I'd have derailed the train before I'd have let you go away." He stopped and looked ill at ease, taking his hand away from my face and stepping back a pace, though still retaining my hand in his other one. He laughed embarrassedly. "I've rehearsed this moment for weeks now, going over and over all I'd say to you and thinking of how romantic it would be. Yet now I find there's no easy way for a man to declare himself to a girl. I have no idea if you could learn to love me. If you'd ever want to marry me."

"Oh, Jon, I am deeply, deeply fond of you," I said all in a rush, moved by his earnest simplicity. "I don't know what to say to you."

"Say yes."

I turned from him a little and looked out over the mountains. For once, I was too agitated to appreciate their ever-changing beauty. I had been proposed to before, but when my would-be suitors discovered I was quietly determined to complete my training as an architect, the offers had been awkwardly withdrawn. But Jon *knew* I was an architect and that I intended to pursue my career with all the strength and ability the good Lord saw fit to give me. We'd discussed our philosophies many times during our rambles. He'd sincerely applauded my intentions and said he didn't see any reason why a woman as clever as myself couldn't combine home and career should she ever marry.

I suddenly felt an almost overwhelming flow of gratitude. Jon was a fine man, a handsome man, happy and fulfilled in his own work. I liked him immensely. What more wonderful thing could happen to a girl than receiving a marriage proposal from such a man on Christmas Eve?

But I just didn't feel the wild rush of happiness I had always anticipated feeling. I knew that had I loved Jon, I certainly would have. Was I a child to expect ecstatic joy? Was not a marriage based on genuine friendship and mutual respect more to be desired than one where love was present and the more-lasting qualities were not? I felt love—I could not deny it—for Anthony Richmond, but I hated his bland superiority while he scoffed at my ambition to establish myself as an architect. But I had no wish to think of Anthony Richmond and pushed him resolutely from my mind.

"Minerva, I've quite taken you unaware. I assumed that you realized I was falling in love with you. Perhaps you just thought me being politely attentive to a guest in my father's house. Forgive me. I have been carried away by my desire to have an understanding with you on Christmas Eve."

I turned back to face him, putting my hand up briefly to brush snow from his blond hair. "No, Jon, it isn't that, although I admit I wasn't really prepared for your proposal. I suppose I have been dimly aware you were becoming fond of me, as I have been of you."

"Minerva, remember what you told me of the men you've known? How they seem to regard you as a freak because you aspire to a profession. Surely it's unnecessary for me to remind you that I'd be proud to acknowledge my wife was clever enough to pursue a career. I would never try to make you over into my servant . . ."

"I know that, Jon. It *isn't* necessary for you to tell me. I have always known you aren't the kind of man who seeks assurance of his own manhood by dominating a woman who loves him, like . . . well, never mind that. In fact, I'm quite sure we'd have a very contented life together."

"Then you will marry me?"

"I didn't mean that. Oh, Jon, forgive me. I hadn't meant for you to take that statement as consent," I said in confusion. "I must have time to think about it. I might . . ." Suddenly, I looked up at him, my confusion clearing a little. I sounded like a coy and false maiden, following the proscribed ritual for well-bred young ladies when presented with a marriage proposal. I did not want such a false role. Jon and I were friends. I would answer him as a dear friend. Nothing else was thinkable.

"Listen to me, Jon. I don't want to mince about and say, 'Sir, I am not unmindful of the great honor you do me, but . . .' though that's exactly how I feel, very fortu-

nate and humble to have won the . . . the . . . regard . . ."

"Call it 'love' if you're really being honest, Minerva, for
that's what it is," he said, with a smile.

"All right. The *love* of a fine man like you. It's what I
have always wanted. And I couldn't possibly think of a
finer man than you." I stopped and smiled up at him
ruefully. "The fact is," I said, "I guess I'm just like my
more conventional sisters after all, Jon, for I feel I should
love you, too, if I consented to marry you. You know, fireworks and bells when we kiss . . ."

He smiled and drew me back to stand directly in front
of him. "How do you know we wouldn't generate fireworks and bells? We've never even kissed."

"That's true," I said, considering. "And, who knows,
maybe that's what the poets call love after all? The normal attraction of a healthy man and woman."

"Then, the intelligent thing to do would be to give it a
try." He pulled me against his chest in one smooth movement and bent his head to meet my lips. I returned his
kiss freely.

It was lovely. I felt my untried femininity responding
to him with a quiet warmth. He was, after all, a very attractive man. What more could I possibly ask for, I
thought, wanting desperately to feel a fierce consuming
passion for this fine young man. What more could any
woman need?

But as I gently pushed him away, my own rebellious
heart supplied me with an answer. I wanted all that Jon
was and more. I wanted a man who'd make me love him
no matter what. I wanted to love so fiercely, so devotedly
that even when he hurt me I wouldn't be driven away. I
was willing to suffer just to be with such a man. Although

I knew that I had to be free . . . an individual, not just an appendage of my husband . . . still, I wanted my ties to him to be so deep I'd walk through fire to be with him. I wanted to be swept off my feet with love, yet have companionship and respect, too. I wanted . . . entirely too much. I wanted . . . Anthony Richmond. But he was nothing like the husband I'd dreamed of. Jon was. Except that it was Anthony that I loved.

I wished passionately that I could shake some common sense into myself. I was an idiot . . . a masochist to fall in love with a man who looked down on me, thwarted me, made light of the work I so loved and, moreover, didn't care a twig about me. Likely he'd be giving Clarice an engagement ring for Christmas. What was he to me after all? I would put my crazy infatuation for him away from me. It was *not* love. I would not *let* it be love. And when I'd gotten over my infatuation for him, perhaps I would learn to love this fine man who was standing here, humbly offering me his heart.

"Well, Minerva," he said gently, "did you see fireworks and hear bells?"

I shook my head regretfully. "It was the nicest thing I've ever done, though," I said honestly. "Will you give me time to think about it? Be just as you have been to me . . . my very good friend? Let love grow in me if it will?"

He smiled a bit ruefully. "I'd hoped for a bit more than that, I have to admit. But I'm happy you haven't flatly said no at least. You're right of course. I would not want you to promise yourself to me if you'd the slightest reservation about it. And, after all, that which grows slowly endures."

"Jon, you are truly fine," I said softly. "I honestly hope I *do* fall in love with you. I would want it to endure."

I thought of the way I felt about Anthony Richmond. Indeed, I almost hated him most of the time. Yet, honesty forced me to admit to myself that from the first moment I'd met him, I'd wanted to be with him. I was ridiculously happy when he was expected to supper, even when all he did was to direct pointed remarks at me across the table. I delighted in the way he looked and held his head and in his proud carriage and broad shoulders. I'd even wondered shamelessly, it seemed to me since he was Clarice's, what it would be like to be cradled against his strong chest. The feeling had been there almost from the first moment I'd seen him. It hadn't grown slowly. Perhaps the cure of my infatuation would be as swift. I earnestly hoped so.

Jon pulled a small box from his pocket and opened it to show me a lovely diamond ring. "I had hoped to give this to you for Christmas, Minerva. Perhaps you'll accept it for your birthday, May fourteenth, isn't it?"

"Perhaps, Jon," I said, without conviction. "Whatever should happen, though, I want to thank you for your love and regard. I truly needed to know there were men in the world secure enough in their own manhood that they could let their wives grow to the limit of their capacities."

We walked back through the wintry fairyland, arriving at the Bosworth house just as Anthony Richmond and Clarice returned from a sleigh ride. No doubt *she'd* accepted the engagement ring he'd likely offered her, I thought miserably.

But after a buffet supper, as we trimmed the tree, I saw no sign of a ring on Clarice's finger. And at nine o'clock, Anthony bowed politely and said his good-byes, promising to be back early in the morning to accompany the family to church and then join in Christmas dinner with the Bosworths.

My gift from Jon the next morning was a box of a dozen lace handkerchieves wrapped with a lavender sachet. He watched with a slight smile as I unwrapped them and thanked him. His eyes seemed to signal me a tender message of regret that we weren't announcing our engagement to the family.

Anthony Richmond arrived with his arms full of gifts. Annette, already in a state of delirium over the tree and gifts, descended on him excitedly, calling him her woolly bear and demanding to be allowed to help distribute the presents. Anthony was a great favorite with Annette, though she was normally a somewhat reserved little girl.

Anthony had brought Annette a doll's cook stove which sent her into an immediate ecstasy and made her forget all about distributing his other gifts.

"Greedy child," he said with a laugh and, before George could take his greatcoat, presented Jon with a pipe, Mr. Bosworth and Bill with wool mufflers, Mary with a pretty pocketbook and George, who had an incurable sweet tooth, with a big box of store chocolates. For Alice, Clarice and myself, there were three identical volumes of Tennyson's poetry.

And for me, there was a wild, soaring joy. He had *not* given Clarice an engagement ring!

The night of the masquerade ball, New Year's Eve, was clear and star-spangled after a snow that had lasted for days, shutting the mountain passes and piling mountains of sparkling white on the housetops of Bellefonte. The little town nestled among its foothills, still and icy, as if it had been a Swiss town. All over the community, sleighs were being brought around and folks were dressing in their best creations which had been kept a great dark secret. The men grumbled that it was a lot of foolishness thought up by the women, but I noticed that Bill Tyndall, studiously draping a sheet over one shoulder to approximate Julius Caesar's toga, was hard put to keep his eyes from dancing.

The ball was being held as a benefit for the Undine Fire Company which desperately needed a new engine. Almost everyone in town would attend.

Certainly everyone in the Bosworth household, including Annette and George and Mary. But as the sleigh couldn't conveniently carry all of us, Jon and Annette and I insisted on walking. Since we all had warm boots, the Tyndalls consented, and we set out briskly toward the center of town and the new Bush Arcade which had a fine ballroom on the third floor.

It was a magic night with the New Year waiting to start and the whole world bright and sparkling and clean. Sleighs with jingling bells and laughing people kept passing us, some offering rides, but we waved back and declined, saying we were enjoying the walk. Anything could happen on such a night, I thought ecstatically. I was on my way to a ball, almost like Cinderella. Indeed, my well-worn green moire had been transformed just as Cinderella's rags had. I had trimmed it lavishly with ivy and holly and had made for myself a sort of crown built around a miner's lamp which Bill had obtained for me. My costume was to represent the Spirit of Christmas Present for Mr. Dickens' *Christmas Carol* had become very popular in the twenty years since his death.

The arcade was decorated gorgeously and agleam with gas lamps. There was an enormous Christmas tree and a table laden with food and drink. As the guests arrived, the room took on the look of a fantastic aviary with brightly plumed birds never before seen on earth.

Mr. Meek, dressed in his usual old business suit, but whimsically wearing a pair of angel's wings, stood near the entrance, smiling benignly or sardonically, depending upon whether he was gazing at a Republican or a Democrat, his pencil and tablet at the ready to record details of the more imaginative costumes. For the life of me, I didn't think there'd be one newspaper reader in all of Bellefonte who hadn't seen everything firsthand.

I recognized few people for most of the crowd, entering fully into the spirit of the occasion, were costumed and masked. The exception was Mr. Grant Roberts who was there in his usual business suit, disdaining, no doubt, to play the child and dress up. His wife, too, was dressed in the same quiet gown she'd worn to the Tyndalls' the first night I'd been in Bellefonte. She avoided my eye, embarrassed, I suppose, by our last encounter. I wondered how she had recognized me and realized Annette, who was holding my hand, had removed her mask the better to see all that was happening. Since I was considerably shorter than either Clarice or Alice, she'd have assumed my identity. Who else was likely to have been with the Tyndalls' daughter?

My dance card was rapidly filled as were those of all the ladies. Jon, preening himself in his Davy Crockett costume, claimed me for the first, shooing Annette off to join her mother.

"Are you enjoying yourself, Fair Ghost?" he said lightly. "I only hope you'll go on haunting me forever."

"Oh, Jon, you're so nice. And so is this whole town," I

cried. "It will be terribly hard returning to Philadelphia when the house is done."

"You won't be returning to Philadelphia," he said with conviction. "By the time the house is complete, you'll have very sensibly made up your mind to marry me."

"You promised we'd just be friends for now, Jon," I said, a bit uncomfortably.

"And so we are. So we shall always be, no matter what happens."

We danced the first two numbers when a new partner came to claim me. He was dressed in a short tunic with sandals that must have been extremely uncomfortable on such a cold night as well as being somewhat daring, I thought. He wore a gilt helmet and a short sword and I assumed he represented Alexander the Great, Conqueror of the World. I looked down at my dance card and saw that he had indeed signed it that way. As he swept me into his arms, his familiar sardonic laugh gave him away as Anthony Richmond.

"How very appropriate your costume is," I said dryly.

"I knew you'd say that," he said complacently. "Yours suits you almost as well as mine does me."

He was maddeningly conceited, I thought, gritting my teeth, and he had a facility of saying things to me that I never knew exactly how to take. Had he meant the color of my dress was becoming to me? Or, and more likely with him, I was sure, that its overdecorated and shining condition was like me? Or my work? Why did I even pay attention to anything he said, I asked myself fiercely. I was always at a disadvantage with him. Always on the defensive in one way or another, even when he was just being conversational. I seemed always to be expecting another of his lightning barbs.

The orchestra changed tempo, swinging into a polka. My partner, too, rapidly changed tempo. I pulled away from him, achingly aware of his proximity when he'd advanced in the dance, and I, taken unaware, had not retreated fast enough.

"I can't polka," I cried. "I am sorry."

"Nonsense," he said, pulling me back into place. "It's easy. Just follow me."

I fell over his rapidly advancing feet which further increased my agitation. "Let me go!" I cried frantically, feeling his hands, those big, capable hands, at either side of my waist. He only laughed, maneuvering my body with his hands tightly at my waist. He whirled me, then, as we reached the corner of the ballroom, and I felt my feet fly out from under me, my legs dragging leadenly against his. I struggled to regain my footing, feeling myself red with embarrassment and anger. But he advanced too rapidly in the rhythm of the dance, stepping down hard on my foot, twisting my ankle cruelly. I cried out and pitched against him as I fell.

"Now you've done it," I said angrily. "I *told* you I couldn't polka. I've really sprained my ankle, and it's all your fault."

He saw at last that I was really incapable of standing erect. Sobering, he lowered me gently to a chair at the edge of the dance floor. I was acutely and painfully aware of the stares of two matronly ladies who'd been watching our wild cavort and Anthony's shamelessly bare legs.

"I'm sorry, Minerva. I didn't mean to hurt you," he began miserably.

"I know that. But you did. Because you're too pigheaded and puffed up with your own exalted person to listen to anyone else," I said through teeth gritted against pain. "You just didn't care that my ineptitude was embarrassing to me. Indeed, you probably enjoyed making me appear foolish."

"If you've finished reading me out, I'll fetch Jon," he said imperturbably. "I suppose your ankle should be attended to."

He stalked off, leaving me feeling foolish and angry with myself, too. I wasn't usually so nasty when someone was tendering an apology. Why did he bring out the worst in me?

In a few minutes, he was back with Jon and Clarice, who'd been dancing with her brother, in tow. She was a vision of unrumpled loveliness dressed as Guinevere.

"I saw you stumble, Minerva, dear," she said sweetly. "Really, darling, how *could* you have been so clumsy?"

I would have liked to wring her beautiful neck, but it was Anthony Richmond who really angered me. He stood beside Clarice, smiling his superior smile. And all the time, it had been *his* fault.

Jon knelt in front of me, all professional concern. He examined my ankle and shook his head. "It is a rather serious sprain, Minerva. I'll have to bind it up immediately or it'll swell."

"Oh, really, Jon?" I cried in disappointment. "Can't I just sit here? Stay off it all evening?"

"You heard Jon, Minerva," Clarice purred. "It will swell. You'd best go home and right to bed."

"I'm sorry, but I have to agree with her, Minerva," Jon said reluctantly. "Even if I had my bag here to treat you immediately, the foot should be elevated. Believe me, you'll be much happier tomorrow if you listen to me tonight."

"I shall miss the party," I said childishly.

"I know and I'm sorry, but there will be others."

I sighed and forced a rueful smile. Jon looked woebegone, and even Anthony seemed a little subdued. "I suppose, then, someone had better help me home," I said.

"Anthony, have Richard Langley bring the sleigh around. He is not dancing just now and won't mind at all. You and I will have to carry Minerva down the stairs. Her ankle mustn't bear her weight or it will swell before I can bandage it."

Anthony strode off to speak to Richard Langley.

"You'll have to return the sleigh, Jon, after you've seen Minerva home," Clarice said. "It's much too early for the rest of us to go now and too far for us to walk."

"It wasn't too far for us to walk down here," Jon said in a rare burst of irritability. "But, never mind, I'll take George along to drive the sleigh back. I'll stay with Minerva."

"George is having entirely too good a time. Besides, do you think it would be quite *proper* for you to be alone with a young unmarried woman for several hours, dear?"

"Oh, Clarice, sometimes you are almost too much to bear," Jon said in exasperation. "All right. I won't disturb anyone. I'll take her home, treat her ankle and drive the sleigh back here. Then I shall *walk* back to be with her. Whether *you* think it's proper or not."

Clarice sniffed and turned away, her purpose accomplished. She didn't really care that Jon would be alone with me. It was simply that she was afraid *her* indolence would be disturbed if she had to walk home. But my palm was itching to connect with the pretty, rose-petal cheek. She had been insinuating and insulting. What did Anthony Richmond *see* in the spoiled girl? He was welcome to her. And the real question was, what did *I* see in *him* when he obviously had no discernment about female character? I could not help but laugh bitterly at myself. I was nearly as conceited as he to think that. Who was I to say *my* character was superior to Clarice's? And that was surely what I had been implying by judging her.

We finally reached the Bosworth house. I had thought Anthony Richmond or, perhaps, Richard Langley might volunteer to drive along and help get me upstairs, then drive the sleigh back, but Jon, stung by Clarice's selfishness, hadn't asked them. He had a stubborn streak when angered. Accordingly, when we reached home, he carried me upstairs and set me on the edge of my bed. He strode to the closet, pulled out my nightgown and robe and handed them to me.

"Now, young lady, I'll leave you alone to get undressed and into your night things. I'm sure you'll be able to manage although it wouldn't have hurt my charming little sister to come along and help you. I should have hunted up Alice."

"No, I'm glad you didn't. I would have hated spoiling her evening," I said.

He smiled approvingly. "You're a nice person, Minerva. But you'll not fare as well in life as Clarice." He touched my cheek lightly, then left the room.

As I struggled out of my costume and into my gown and robe, I reflected ruefully that he was right. Clarice would have everything her little heart desired. Money, a house, leisure and . . . Anthony. Then, ashamed of my jealousy, I smoothed down my robe and called Jon back in to bind up my ankle.

He finished deftly. Indeed, it did feel better.

"Look, Minerva, I'll not be long returning the sleigh.

And I'll lock the door behind me. Don't put any weight on that ankle. I'll take a few pastries from the refreshment table for us and we'll see the New Year in together after all."

"I'd really feel better if you stayed," I protested. "I hate making you miss all the fun."

"It won't *be* any fun without you. I'll be back as soon as possible."

He leaned over and kissed my forehead, then left the room. I heard him descend the stairs, cross the hall, open and close the door, locking it behind him. In a few seconds, I heard the bells as he turned the sleigh about and started down Spring Street.

Jon had lit the gas log in the fireplace before he left and, lulled by its warmth and mesmerizing flicker, I fell into a fitful doze. I dreamed about Anthony Richmond and his Alexander the Great costume. He kept forcing me to dance by lunging at my ankles with his short sword, laughing sardonically as he did so.

I awoke with a start, hearing tinkling glass. I sat up in bed, my senses straining for a further sound. The house was completely quiet except for the slow ticking of the clock in the hall. There was no sound from outside, either, on the cold, windless night. Everyone from this end of town was at the Bush Arcade awaiting the advent of the New Year. I had doubtless been dreaming . . . perhaps it was Anthony's sword in my dream that had seemed to make the sound. Or an icicle falling from the roof outside. Still, I was suddenly aware of my vulnerability alone here in the house. What if the sound I had heard had been someone breaking a window?

I lay motionless, listening with all my concentration, all my half-forgotten fears of the autumn surfacing again.

Perhaps it was Jon coming back, I thought fleetingly, but knew he'd have stomped up on the porch in his usual way, knocking the worst of the snow from his boots before coming into the front hall.

Then, from the library below, I heard a faint sound. Someone was moving across the room!

I stared frantically around the room for something to support me for I knew my ankle would scarcely bear my weight. My umbrella was just inside the closet, and I stepped from the bed as silently as possible on my good foot, holding onto pieces of furniture as I made my way to the closet.

I opened the door, grabbing the umbrella and gratefully putting my weight on it. My heart was beating frantically from the effort of getting across the room quietly, incapacitated as I was, and from simple fear. After all, there was someone in this house who was moving quietly to avoid being heard. Someone who knew I was alone and unprotected here! Someone who'd doubtless been at the Bush Arcade and seen me being carried down the stairs and placed in the sleigh. It might have been anyone in town.

I stumped painfully toward the door of my room, feeling a bit more confident now with my umbrella to assist me in getting around. I jerked the door open and went out into the hall, realizing only too well that I was effectively cut off from escape because of my injured ankle. Even if I'd been able to get down the steep back stairs, the intruder would hear me and be upon me before I could get away. Or, supposing I were able to maneuver the spiral stairs, where could I get help tonight with everyone away and the snow heavy on the ground? My bare feet would be frozen before I walked half a mile, even supposing that were possible with my ankle so badly injured.

The only alternative seemed to be bluffing, I thought. I forced myself to think calmly. Then, proud of my own subterfuge, I stood at the top of the stairs and called.

"Is that you, Jon? You *said* you'd be right back, but that was really fast." I smiled in the dimly lit hall. *That* would inform the intruder that Jon was expected back momentarily.

There was no answer from the darkened first floor. Nothing but the inexorable tick of the clock, so comforting when all the family was here, almost menacing now with a lurking stranger below.

Suddenly, I heard quiet but purposeful footsteps moving across the library and into the downstairs hall.

"Who's there?" I said, my voice betraying my fear.

There was no answer except an almost imperceptible break in the footfalls. They came purposefully toward the stairs. I heard the first step creak as the intruder set foot on it. I could see only a dark mass for the only light in the house was the tiny flicker of the gas log from my bedroom.

"Answer me. Who are you?" I cried, falling back, letting the umbrella hold my weight.

Silently and relentlessly, the figure moved up the stairs.

I fell back hastily toward the rear of the hall and the service stairs. Already, my pursuer was gaining on me, handicapped as I was by my injured ankle. I'd never get away! Still, the service stairs were at hand. Perhaps, perhaps I might get down to the kitchen, hide from the intruder until Jon arrived. But, what if he were delayed? I was clumsy and slow. The mysterious dark figure who stalked me might overtake me long before I could find a hiding place below.

But what if he thought I'd gone down to the kitchen when in fact I'd gone on to the third floor? Maybe I could hide up there until Jon came. Maybe, and I prayed it was so, he wouldn't know about the slave room and I could elude him long enough for Jon to get back. So thinking, I threw my umbrella down the kitchen stairs. The sound would make him think I *had* started down that way and perhaps lost my footing. As silently as I was able, wincing at the pain in my ankle, I slipped down the back hall to the attic entrance.

I heard my pursuer, evidently deceived by my throwing the umbrella, start down the back stairs. Under cover of his slight noise, I pulled the attic stair door open and closed it silently behind me. I crawled up the rough stairs on my hands and knees, scarcely breathing in an effort to hide my whereabouts. Oh, God, let him not know about the slave room, I prayed frantically, tears starting in my eyes.

I reached the top of the stairs, my nightgown torn from catching under my knees. Quietly, I opened the closet door and groped among the trailing garments for the leather strap on the floor. Finally grasping it, I pulled the trapdoor up and frantically shook the garments back into place to conceal it. Breathing in short, shallow gasps, I pulled the closet door shut behind me and let myself painfully down onto the ladder, my hands clutching the old clothes in an effort to take the weight off my ankle.

It was in vain. There was no way to get down the rough ladder without putting my full weight onto the injured ankle. It hurt so badly I nearly cried out, but I knew my life might well depend on my silence, so I bit

my lip until I felt warm blood well into my mouth as I
lowered myself into the aperture. Tears were running
down my cheeks before I reached the bottom. I dropped
in a heap on the floor, not daring to sit on the bedstead
for fear of creaking springs. My ankle throbbed painfully
and the room around me was pitch black, oppressive, the
walls seeming to lean in upon me. It was like a grave,
holding me helpless and unable to escape. Yet, outside in
the great, empty, echoing house, the terror was greater,
more real than the choking fear I felt here in the black,
black depths of the slave room. I pressed my hands across
my mouth, tasting blood and dirt, willing myself to be silent and listen, to gauge where my pursuer was, not to
give way to terrified screaming.

He had discovered I'd not gone downstairs now, and
had come back up to the second floor, moving with less
stealth through all the rooms. I heard him shutting closet
doors, rummaging about in all the bedrooms. I shut my
eyes and imagined him peering into the depths of the
closets, kneeling to look under the beds and even in the
huge old armoires in the back bedrooms. At last, satisfied
that I was not hiding on the second floor, I heard him
open the stair door to the attic. I buried my face in my
arms to keep from screaming. He'd find me! I knew it!
I remembered childhood nightmares when I dreamed
wild, red Indians from the western states were pursuing
me and I'd been able to find no place to hide from them.
I'd always awakened screaming, my father's comforting
arms about me, soothing me, telling me it was only a
dream after all and I was quite safe in my father's house.
How I wished I could wake from this situation safe and
comforted and happy.

The steps came upward. He'd find me now. I should

have pulled the trapdoor down behind me. Perhaps then he wouldn't have noticed its presence. As it was, he'd surely look in the closet, see the yawning black at his feet and know there was a hiding place beneath the floor.

The closet door was pulled open. I could hear his every movement, see the faint light from the star-lit night shining through the attic windows behind my pursuer's head. He stood there a long moment, a dark mass against the lighter dark of the attic. I nearly fainted from fear and nausea.

Then, from far below, I heard the front door slam. A moment later, someone was loping up the front steps, calling my name. I recognized Jon's voice but dared not call out to him and give away my presence to the malevolent presence above. At least help was near, though. Thank God, Jon had come.

The dark figure whirled about and ran swiftly and silently down the attic stairs. Beneath me, now, I could hear him going on downward into the kitchen. He passed Jon, using the back stairs and would get away safely. But at least, thank God, I was safe! I dragged myself back to the ladder and tried to climb out of the slave room, but now that the immediate danger was past, I could not stand the pain of the injured ankle. I collapsed against the ladder and filled my lungs with air.

"Here I am, Jon. Help me! Oh, for heaven's sake, help me!" I screamed. I tilted the little table over and picked up the candle, scrambling for the heavy glass candleholder. When I had it in my grasp, I began banging on the tabletop with it to further add to the noise I was making. I hoped Jon could hear me through the thick walls.

In a moment, I heard him running up the attic stairs. "Minerva, Minerva, where are you?" he called.

"I'm here, Jon, in the slave room," I cried, tears running down my face. "Thank God you're here."

I saw his kind face at the aperture above, lit by the lamp he carried, and then, on a long sigh of pain and relief, I fainted dead away.

CHAPTER 7

After the events of New Year's Eve, there could no longer be the slightest doubt that I was the target of very real malice.

I had been badly shaken by the incident in the slave room and moreover, my ankle had been further injured by climbing down the ladder. I stayed in bed for more than a week, for Jon insisted the injury wouldn't heal without complete rest. The days in bed gave me ample opportunity to think about all that had happened to me. Yet, after mulling endlessly over the attacks, I still couldn't make any sense of them. And, finally, realizing my brooding and worrying was making me nervy and ill, I simply quit. Jon had gone to the sheriff on New Year's day after finding a library window had indeed been smashed in. He reported to me and the family that he'd told the sheriff everything that had happened since I'd arrived in Bellefonte, stressing our suspicions that the disappearance of Mrs. Bosworth and the death at the mine might possibly be connected with all that had happened to me. The sheriff promised to investigate and to keep a close eye on the Bosworth house as long as I was there. It seemed totally inadequate, Jon said impotently, but I realized only too well there was little else the sheriff could do. We had none but the flimsiest of motives or evidence. Only the constant apprehension I felt now seemed real.

I was finally able to walk with a cane, although the weather outside was too severe, the boardwalks too treacherously icy for me to get out.

Then one day late in January when I'd finally discarded the cane, a letter arrived from the *American Architect and Builder* magazine! Mr. Bosworth brought it to me in the sun porch whose walls had risen while I was confined to bed. His eyes were shining with anticipation as he dropped it in my lap.

"I'll bet it's an announcement of the contest winners," he said. "Oh, Minerva, open it. Do you think you might have won?"

My hands were trembling too badly. I handed it back to him. "You read it, sir. Hurry."

He tore the end off the envelope and extracted a sheet of paper. "My Dear M. J. Stewart," he read slowly, then, his handsome face lighting to happy excitement, "This letter is to inform you that you have been named the winner in our dwelling-design contest. The panel of judges found your design fresh and original, although borrowing heavily from established architectural styles.

"We understand the house will be constructed in the spring of 1891 and are eagerly looking forward to having a photograph of its interior and exterior for featuring in a future issue of our magazine. In the event that you should not be able to complete the house by July 1, the award will be forfeited and the contest reopened.

"Congratulations on your winning design. We look forward to hearing from you soon. Sincerely, Editor, *American Architect and Builder* magazine."

I screamed with delight, jumping from my chair to hug Mr. Bosworth. "I can't believe it. I honestly can't believe it," I cried.

He patted my shoulder and hugged me back, as delighted as I. "*I* do," he said gleefully. "I always knew you were talented. Even if I hadn't trusted Bill and Alice's assessment of your ability, those designs spoke for themselves. This will be the most livable, attractive house built in Bellefonte since the early days."

I could only laugh and read the letter over and over. I'd won other awards, obscure little contests sponsored by lumberyards in the Philadelphia area, but this was different. Architects all over the country read the magazine that had sponsored this one. Moreover, I knew, women's magazines and other popular publications picked up such prize-winning designs. The winning of this contest would make my reputation! When I returned to Philadelphia, there would be more work than I could handle.

Mr. Bosworth stood there laughing and congratulating me over and over. Suddenly, I felt a great affection for the old man. How generous he was to be happy about my triumph! To me, whose own family was gone, it brought a poignant gratitude.

"We must tell the others," he said. "I can't wait to see Bill and Alice's face. They never expected when they gave you permission to submit the design that it would make their house famous."

"Oh, you don't think they'll mind?" I said, suddenly apprehensive, clutching the precious letter. "When they told me to go ahead and send it, they naturally thought my chance of winning was slim. Perhaps they won't want all the publicity in view of all that's happened here . . ."

"Won't want all *what* publicity?" Bill Tyndall said with a smile as he appeared at the door of the sun-room, his greatcoat and hat still on.

"Minerva's house has won the contest, Bill!" Mr. Bosworth said. "Isn't that wonderful?"

Bill Tyndall's pleasant and dignified face took on a look of delight. "That's *absolutely* marvelous," he cried. "I am delighted to have my own and Alice's judgment proved so right."

"Then you won't mind having the house featured in magazine write-ups?" I asked.

"Of course not. I can't think of anything I'd rather have happen. It will certainly make this country sit up and take notice that ability in such fields as building and architecture aren't exclusive to the male of the species. High time the talent and genius of women are allowed to grace our lives. You well know I've always thought too much of it was like lights under bushels." He pulled his hat off and glanced back into the kitchen from which the new sunporch would open. "Have you told Alice yet?"

"No, the letter just came. You and your father-in-law are the first to know," I said, still glowing from his words.

He smiled and with an inquiring-for-permission lift of his eyebrows, took the letter from my hand. "Come on, then, let's tell her." And pulling me by the hand, he went into the front hall.

"Alice. Alice, darling. Come down here this minute, we have the most marvelous news for you."

Word of my triumph spread quickly. Mr Meek came to the house a few days later to do an interview about my winning the contest. He scribbled rapidly as I told him about my early training at the Philadelphia Normal Art School and at the Franklin Institute and of the frustration of not being able to obtain a position with an established firm.

"You'll have no trouble now," he said. "Woman or not, I imagine there'll be plenty of firms wanting to have you as an associate."

"I hope so," I said. "All I have to do now is to be certain the house is finished before July 1."

"Is that a stipulation of the contest?"

"Yes. Otherwise, it will be reopened."

He scribbled again. I stared at the flying pencil uneasily. Perhaps it would be better if that information weren't published, I thought. I'd had enough trouble since I came to Bellefonte to build this house. Suppose *someone,* realizing what completing the house before July first meant to me, decided to cause me problems and delays. I thrust the thought away as if it were something unclean, realizing unhappily that the only one who would want to see me lose the first place award was Anthony Richmond. All the other accidents that had occurred had nothing whatsoever to do with the contest. I could not bear to think that *he* was behind them.

Mr. Meek finished with his notes and stood up, reaching for his old felt hat. "Congratulations, young lady," he said brusquely. "Real feather in Bellefonte's cap to have an architect of your stature building a house here. I'll be anxious to have it finished so I can photograph it."

"Perhaps you could make a copy for me to send to the magazine, Mr. Meek," I suggested.

"Be glad to"—his bright little eyes gleamed wickedly— "*if* you'll give my paper a credit line."

I laughed and stood up to show him to the door. "I most certainly will," I said. "And thank you for doing the story."

The story came out in the next evening's paper. It was

very flattering to me and calculated to pique the public curiosity about the Tyndalls' new house.

A few days later, as I walked toward the center of town, a short, burly figure stepped arrogantly in front of me. I fell back, meeting the eyes of the man who'd so peremptorily confronted me. They were the agate-blue eyes of Tam Whitney.

"So, now the house you're building for Bill Tyndall is a prize winner, no less," he spat bitterly at me.

I was completely taken aback by the suddenness with which the little miner had accosted me, but I drew myself up and stared him down, angered that he should use his difference with Tyndall to so rudely confront me.

"Thank you for your interest, Mr. Whitney," I said with icy irony. "I believe it is."

"You needn't thank me for my interest, Miss Stewart. I can tell you that," he said with a mirthless laugh. "For it isn't offered in a friendly manner."

"I'm well aware of that from your tone," I said, "and for the life of me, I can't understand why you've developed such a wrong-headed aversion to Mr. Tyndall. From all I've been able to see since arriving in Bellefonte, he's working day and night to correct injustices to the miners. He has suffered a very great deal over the death of your son and is determined that such accidents will be avoided as long as he's the manager of the Nittany Mine."

"Oh, *he's* suffered, has he? Well, he'll learn about suffering before I'm satisfied," the little man snapped, his blue eyes gleaming fanatically. "And nothing you nor my old lady can say will ever change my mind."

"I'm sorry for that, Mr. Whitney. I think perhaps *time* will. You'll come to realize that what Bill Tyndall promises will come to pass. I know that he's very angry over the delay in the payment of the insurance money to your son's children, for instance. He's employed a lawyer to take the insurance company to court, and they're both quite certain they'll get it. And you can't be ignorant of the safety policies he's been initiating at the mine . . ."

"Why don't you just get out of this? It isn't your problem. Take your prize-winning design and go build it in Philadelphia. You're liable to get hurt," he broke in vehemently.

I felt a shudder move over my body in spite of myself. His tone was so threatening. And so many near tragedies had already happened to me and my designs. "I don't like your tone, Mr. Whitney," I said with a boldness I was far from feeling. "I suggest very strongly that you re-examine your misguided feelings about Mr. Tyndall. I pity you, indeed I do, and feel your sorrow, but I must admit, if you were *my* employee and so persistently wished me ill, I'd be tempted to fire you."

"Don't you stand here and preach to me, you little female," he cried, clenching his fists and advancing on me a step. "I don't need the likes o' you to tell me the right and wrong o' things. I've got the Good Book for my guide, and it offers better advice than you'll ever give."

"I've no doubt of *that*, Mr. Whitney," I said more humbly, realizing that I had, indeed, been preaching at him. "What passage in particular did you have in mind?"

"'An eye for an eye, and a tooth for a tooth . . .'" he said, spitting venomously at my feet. And with a last bitter smile, he turned and stalked away.

There were two more fires during the winter and the people of Bellefonte worked harder than ever to raise the money for a new fire engine. It was finally delivered and paid for in mid-February while a pair of sturdy horses were fitted with harness to haul it. It was a day of jubilation for the entire town and, at the cake and ice-cream social the Undine Fire Company had to launch the new engine, Anthony Richmond was teased thoroughly about the town's new fire-protection machine.

"Won't do you any good to be burning buildings anymore, Richmond," the firemen called jocularly across the crowded Arcade ballroom, "we'll be able to put 'em out before they've had a chance to do much damage now."

Anthony seemed to accept the ribbing in good part. The truth was that fire was a very real danger in the little town with its buildings close together and the new gas-heating plant coming into operation. The old folks grumbled and said there'd never been so many fires when they relied on the old kitchen and parlor stoves to heat their homes. These new-fangled furnaces were to blame. I knew there was a kernel of truth in what they said. Too many of the older homes were not really adapted to adding new central-heating systems with old fireplace or kitchen chimneys as flues. If the furnace installers would only realize the need to thoroughly inspect the old chimneys, even build new ones when necessary, the occurrence of fires would diminish.

Or so I told myself. I stared across the room at Anthony who was sitting with Clarice as usual although that didn't prevent her from flirting with two other of her many swains. They teased Anthony about burning down houses in order to drum up more business for himself. The notion was preposterous of course. And yet, someone was trying to drive me away from Bellefonte. That seemed preposterous, too. Whitney? Clarice? Anthony Richmond? Angrily, I shook my head and resolved not to think about the questions that were plaguing me. I could not solve them, but I certainly wasn't about to run away from them. Fortune had finally begun to smile on my career. I'd worked too hard, suffered too much, to give up now. Whoever was trying to frighten me away would find I was not a coward. I was in Bellefonte to build a house, and build it I would. As soon as the ground thawed in the spring.

That happy event occurred sooner than I dared to hope. In mid-February a series of mild days started the ground softening, the snow melting away to join the creeks where the ice was breaking up. There was some danger of flooding for a while by the early clement weather, but then the nights turned cold, allowing the snow to melt a bit more slowly, and the danger was past. But the ground was thawed! And at last, the builder the Tyndalls had engaged announced that he was ready to start the foundation.

We broke ground in early March and work on the house progressed like a song. Or really, more like a symphony with the men working efficiently, each at his own job. The foundation was in and the framing and roof all done before the early warm spell was over. Then snow and freezing rain returned, but the house was under roof. I was at the site early and late, wearing heavy rubber boots and one of old Mr. Bosworth's discarded greatcoats. At first, I was apprehensive as to how the builder, Mr. Boggs, would accept my being constantly on the job. I was afraid he'd think I was meddling and trying to tell him how to do his job, but it was my house, my design, and if things weren't right, I'd feel responsible to the Tyndalls. To my surprise, he accepted my presence matter-of-factly as did the men.

"It's a good house, miss," he said to me. "I've never built one like it before, but the construction's sound. It'll last." And I heard him tell Bill Tyndall when he came to see how the work was progressing. "She knows *her* job and mine as well."

I was inordinately pleased by his words and the genuine respect in his tone. I could do it! I was proving I could design and build fine houses. The men didn't resent building a house designed by a woman, and when they saw that I didn't expect to be helped over piles of lumber, they stopped even paying attention to me when I was at the site. I was just another person doing a job.

Matters seemed to be improving at the mine, too. At dinner one night, Bill reported that he'd finally bullied Mr. Roberts into giving the miners a raise bringing them up to the hitherto unheard of salary of seventy cents a day!

"It's an outrage that I had to threaten to quit before he'd grant it, too," he said, carving angrily at the ham. "Imagine men working like dogs from their boyhood just to keep body and soul precariously together. They develop sciatica and lung disease while still young men for less than a dollar a day! It was like pulling teeth to get even a small raise for them, but it's a beginning. I'll better their lot or I'll quit, and Roberts knows it." He stopped and lifted his eyebrows comically. "I think he'd have returned to his home in New York City a long time ago if he didn't think I'd give the store away in his absence."

Alice passed the glazed carrots to me, her attention on what her husband was saying. "I don't know why he just doesn't leave everything to you, dear," she said complacently. "You've showed a bigger profit than that rickety old mine ever did before even with your 'philanthropic propensities' as Roberts calls them."

His eyes were grim as he answered her. "Greed, Alice, it's ugly, human greed."

He went on to say that all the rotting timbers had been replaced at the mine and that he'd been investigating the possibility of buying an improved drill for use in case of another cave-in. It was important that better and safer ways to get the coal were developed, he said, for need for it would continue to grow. Although, he said, in time, coal would be used primarily to generate electricity to heat homes. We all expressed disbelief about that, but he only smiled. Then, sobering, he leaned his elbows on the table, his fingertips together and surveyed us over the resultant peak.

"Whatever happens," he said prophetically, "this nation can't afford to build wealth without allowing a corresponding prosperity for the men who do the dirty work of the nation. We can't continue to reap huge profits while men die prematurely from overwork and inadequate nourishment. If we continue to ignore men's welfare, there'll be strikes and violence and world chaos."

I thought of what he said and of the embittered expression Tam Whitney wore. Perhaps, in Bellefonte at least, the violence had already begun.

Work on the house continued to progress well. It seemed that I'd be well within the time limit imposed by the contest rules. There were no further incidents such as had menaced me in the past, and I began to relax. Perhaps the culprit had been Tam Whitney and the raise in pay, the insurance settlement, and the replaced mine timbers had convinced him at last that Bill Tyndall was a man of good will. It seemed as good an explanation as any, and we all breathed easier. The mysterious happenings promised to be one of those things that no one would ever really be able to explain. And I was glad they seemed to stop.

My friendship with Jon continued to grow. Every day I came to respect and admire him more, and although he didn't press me for an answer to his proposal of marriage, I thought about my ultimate decision more and more.

I no longer tried to hide from myself the fact that I was in love with Anthony Richmond. But it was a hopeless love. He cared nothing for me. So I tried to put my mooning after him from my mind and concentrate on learning to think of Jon as a husband.

One evening when George and Mary had gone to prayer meeting and Clarice was with Anthony at the Garmen Opera House, Mr. Bosworth and the Tyndalls decided to go for a walk in the woods to hunt the elusive little arbutus blossoms that bloomed under cover of last year's dried leaves, often before all the snow was gone from the ground. They wanted Jon and me to go, too, but he insisted that the rough terrain was too treacherous for my ankle and said he'd stay and sit with me in the new sun porch until their return.

"I don't think a ramble in the woods would have hurt my ankle one bit," I grumbled as the family moved out of sight down the slope behind the house. "I stand on it all day when I'm working at the house. It doesn't bother me at all."

He smiled wickedly. "I know. It's fine. I just wanted to be alone with you. I thought perhaps you'd have made a decision in my favor about marrying me."

I enjoyed Jon's company, looked forward to his arriving

home from his calls every day or, as he sometimes did, to having him come to the house site to drive me home in his rig. We shared so many of the same enthusiasms and viewpoints that we were beginning to finish each other's sentences. Surely this was the stuff of which the most enduring and successful marriages were made, I told myself, and with my increasing awareness of Jon's fine character and our mutual affection, I determined to push all thoughts of Anthony Richmond from my mind. When he would again offer me his hand on my birthday, I'd accept him.

"I can't wait until May, Minerva," he said as if reading my mind. "I find I'm suffering from a malady that has no medical cure. I watch you and yearn for you and when you smile at me, I think, 'Yes, her smile for me is special; I know it is.'"

"And always will be, Jon," I said, touched by his whimsy.

"Do you think about my proposal?"

"All the time."

"Marriage with me would be a very pleasant thing," he said enticingly, like a charming child offering a bride.

"I'm well aware that it would be."

"Will you say yes, then?"

I smiled and looked at my hands. Why not, I thought. I had been honest with him. He knew I didn't love him. But we had so much to guarantee a good marriage. Yes, I would have him.

I raised my eyes to his and opened my mouth to speak the words of assent he wanted to hear. But suddenly, Anthony Richmond's mocking dark eyes seemed to float across Jon's gentle gray ones as clearly as if it was he who sat on the wicker sofa beside me instead of Jon. How could I marry Jon, a voice within me cried, when it was Anthony that I loved? He despised me, mocked me, insulted me, perhaps even hated me, but my foolish heart was set on him beyond recall.

"What is it, Minerva?" Jon said tenderly, taking my hand.

I blinked back the tears and smiled at him. "It's nothing, Jon, really."

He watched me perceptively. "If you say yes, we can go on a long honeymoon trip as soon as the house is finished. You'll need a good rest for when the design is published, you'll be a busy young woman," he said wooingly.

I leaned forward and, very gently, kissed his cheek. "I'm sorry, Jon. I've only just realized that I can't. I only wish I'd had the courage to admit it to myself last Christmas so that you would not have spent the last months building on the possibility of our marrying. Will you forgive me my cowardice?"

He started to protest, but I placed a finger on his lips.

"It's no use, Jon. Everything you could possibly say to me by way of persuasion I've already said to myself. No doubt it would be the wisest move I'd ever make in my life. Certainly, I've never met anyone I admired, respected and just plain *liked* better than you. I'm a fool to say no to you. But admiration and affection just aren't enough for me. And I suspect, in time, my lack of love would come to hurt you deeply. I would hate myself then. I cannot marry you, Jon."

He stared at me for a long time and then he smiled with an air of resignation.

"I see. I really do see, Minerva. I tried to ignore the impossibility, just as you did. But a blind man could see what is in your eyes for Tony."

I started and stared at him. "Does it really show?" I asked with a sinking heart for I couldn't bear that Anthony Richmond should know what I felt for him.

"Not really. Perhaps I saw it because I was looking for that certain softness in your eyes. I so hoped it would be for me."

"I wish to heaven it could be," I said fervently. "Oh, Jon, why can't it be?"

He leaned forward and kissed my forehead. "I don't suppose anyone will ever figure that out, Minerva," he said sadly.

"I'm so sorry I've hurt you."

"You haven't, my dear. Oh, I *am* hurting. Disappointed. No use denying that. But *you* didn't do it. At least not purposely. And I find it very easy to say, 'Can't we at least be friends?'"

"Oh, I hope we can, Jon. I'd feel very badly indeed if I thought I had to sacrifice our friendship in order to do the honorable thing."

"You haven't. I'll always be your friend. Don't you ever forget it."

I smiled tenderly and took his hand in mine. "There'll be someone in time, Jon. A lovely girl. Good and fine like you. And *she'll* love you the way I do Anthony. Her love will not be hopeless as mine is."

"That is a problem for you, isn't it?" he said thoughtfully. "He seems enthralled by my sister."

"Yes," I agreed miserably. "But I'll be leaving soon. And no one will be the wiser except you."

"You mean Anthony has no suspicion of how you feel?"

"Of course not. That I couldn't bear."

He stared at me for a long moment. "You're a very prideful woman, Minerva. Which is gallant and fine. But perhaps there are times when one should swallow her pride. Anthony is a fine man for all that surface smugness. I can't help but think, though it's painful to me, how much better off he'd be with a wife like you instead of my selfish little sister."

I laughed at that. "How disloyal of you, Jon."

He laughed too. "I suppose it is, but except for having her nose put sharply out of joint for a while, it would be no real loss to Clarice. She'd be better off marrying one of our rich young heirs to an old iron, coal or limestone fortune with lots of money and leisure to entertain her to her selfish little heart's desire. Tony would never be content to be her lapdog for long."

"But, you see, I *do* have my foolish pride," I said ironically.

"Couldn't you swallow it, even to save him from Clarice?"

"Ah, if I thought I could! But he can't stand me. He hates women with brains and ability. I . . . heaven help me . . . perhaps I'm in love enough to give up my career . . . hide my reasoning power to win him . . . but I know it just wouldn't work. To deny the gifts God chose to give one for whatever reason is the greatest sin, I think. And if I did, in the end I'd lose him anyhow for I'd hate myself. And no one can ever truly love you when you hate yourself."

" 'To thine own self be true,' eh?" he said gently.

"Exactly. There's no other way."

He stared at me for a long moment. "You'll be all right, Minerva," he said at last, with admiration. "If you're true to yourself, then you've chosen a wise course, for you're a woman of character and strength. Now let's go meet the family."

On a chilly April morning, the work on the house being purely routine at that point and not needing my presence, I walked downtown to order shellac for the woodwork and floors. On the way back, in spite of the inclement weather, I stopped at Clayton Brown's store where he'd been experimenting with a sort of cone-shaped cookie in which he put ice cream so that one didn't have to use a spoon to eat it. I found the confections delicious and usually succumbed to my passion for them anytime I was downtown.

I had just paid for it and was leaving the store when Anthony Richmond came bustling around the corner and nearly collided with me.

"Why, good morning, Minerva. I hardly recognized you without your charming working costume on," he said, with the faint smile that always irritated me. He sometimes walked over to Curtin Street to see how my house was coming and had seen me in my clumsy boots and Mr. Bosworth's coat. Knowing how revolting I looked in the shabby things with a woolen scarf tied about my head, I knew he meant the remark sarcastically.

"How's the Taj Mahal of Linn Street coming?" I said acidly.

"Oh, finished weeks ago," he said cheerfully.

"Are you out drumming up business now?"

"No, I have more than I can handle. I'll be remodeling the Seminary, the Courthouse, and building two houses this summer. As a matter of fact, I'm thinking of taking on an assistant."

"How nice for you." I finished my cone and wiped my

fingers on my handkerchief. "It's been nice talking to you," I said, "but I have to go now. I want to check on the house before I go home."

He fell into step beside me as I started up Allegheny Street. "I'd like to see the marvel of Bellefonte, too," he said.

"Minerva's Citadel?" I asked, with a short laugh.

"That's no worse than 'The Taj Mahal of Linn Street,'" he countered.

I smiled a bit sheepishly, glad to see I'd stung him, too.

"I can't imagine why you'd want to look at my house unless it's to poke more fun at it," I said, with ill grace. "But come on. I'll take you on a tour."

We stalked along in silence until we reached the crest of the hill where Allegheny Street crossed Curtin. Turning north, we continued toward the house, passing the builder and his crew.

"It's Saturday, miss, and I've decided to give the men a half-day off," he explained. "The house is well ahead of schedule."

"That's fine, Mr. Boggs," I said. "They've been working awfully hard. I'm glad you thought of it."

Anthony and I climbed the heavy slabs of stone I'd ordered for steps and crossed the front porch to open my catty-cornered door. I was silent and uncomfortable, knowing he'd likely make more of his ambiguous comments about my house. I would have liked to slam the door on his face. But at the same time, I yearned to win approval from him, however grudgingly given.

We paused in the wide reception hall. The fireplace was finished and the pine beams I'd specified for the hall ceiling were nearly all in place. The pungent scent of new wood permeated the house.

"The fireplace in the front hall is a nice touch," he said suddenly. "Very welcoming, in fact."

I glanced at him quickly to see if he meant any sarcasm. I couldn't believe he'd grasped the reason for the fireplace so quickly. "Thank you," I managed stiffly, not really knowing how to accept a compliment from him.

He laughed in delight and turned me to face him. "You know, you're really a very beautiful girl when your jaw isn't set as if you'd like to trounce me."

I jerked away quickly. "I wouldn't *set* my jaw if I didn't always feel at a disadvantage with you. You are always so critical."

"*You* are always so defensive."

Suddenly, I felt ridiculous. He was quite right. I *was* always on the defensive with him. Always seeking to justify myself to him. As if I had to. As if I had to justify myself to *anyone*. As I stood in the hallway of my beautiful house, I realized suddenly that the house, my concept, my work, was its own justification. The Tyndalls loved it. As would people who lived in it a hundred years from now. Two hundred! There was no other house like it in Pennsylvania though there'd likely be plenty of imitators when it was pictured in the *American Builder and Architect.* I smiled up at Anthony shamefacedly.

"You're quite right. I am sorry. You *do* raise my hackles and bring out the worst in me."

He was staring down at me with an expression I couldn't read in his dark eyes. "Minerva, you *are* a lovely woman. Why do you feel compelled to do work like this?" he said softly.

"Why do you?" So he'd complimented me and my fireplace only to disarm me for a new attack, I thought angrily.

"Because I've a talent for it. Because I *like* it. It gives me a feeling of real accomplishment to build homes for families."

"That's exactly what I feel," I answered, glad, somehow, that his motives were similar to mine.

"But you would make a wonderful *wife*," he said stubbornly, as if being the one precluded the other. "If you'd only remember a woman's natural function."

My temper, in spite of my good resolutions, exploded into a thousand pieces. "Which, according to the gospel of Mr. Anthony Richmond is to sit, an adoring sycophant at the feet of the man charitable enough to choose me," I stormed. "Well, I have news for you, sir. There are a few men in this world, not many, I grant you, but a few, who don't *need* that kind of adulation from their wives. They wouldn't *expect* their wives to deliberately suppress their own God-given talents because *they* need the illusion that the lordly male is superior. These men have a good, honest, healthy appreciation of their *own* worth and don't *need* to make a woman feel fit for nothing but a drudge, stupid and mindless, in order to bolster their own sagging egos . . ."

Very suddenly, he grabbed me in powerful arms and shut my mouth effectively with a hard, strong, smothering kiss. I was taken by surprise, but fury instantly followed and I struggled against him, beating at his shoulders and chest with all my strength. I tried to pull my face away but he held me fast and to my shame and fury, fireworks started to go off. Worse! I felt exactly like a volcano capped with a parasol. My body and mind throbbed to be held closer still. I felt myself returning his kiss, pressing my lips and body closer to him. His arms relaxed and cradled, lifting me toward his kiss, melting, blissful and floating, exploding until there was nothing in the whole world except him and me and the dear merging.

But just as suddenly as he'd seized me, he released me and held me back at arm's length so that I was left reaching and vulnerable, my face flushed, breath coming in shallow gasps, hair disheveled. He laughed, that hateful, superior laugh that had pursued and goaded me since the day we'd met.

"I thought that was all that ailed you," he said smugly. "You've simply never been kissed until your toes curled up. Such a deprivation leads to all sorts of frustration and bizarre behavior in the female of the species. Even makes her think she might be capable of entering the business world."

I howled then. I simply howled like an enraged beast. If there'd been a length of board in the front hall, I'd likely have brained him once and for all.

"You cad! You vile, unspeakable, villainous, presumptuous cad! Get out of my house!"

"It isn't *your* house," he drawled.

"Well, get out of it anyhow. And I never want to see you again. I can't *wait* to leave Bellefonte. Kindly send word when you're expected at the Bosworths', and I'll make it a point to be elsewhere . . ."

"I'll not be visiting the Bosworths again," he said smoothly. "Clarice and I have agreed not to continue our friendship."

"And because she jilted you, you decided to do the bizarre lady architect a favor and kiss her," I stormed, more angry with myself than with him by the surge of joy that rose inside me when he said he and Clarice were parting company. I could have slapped myself. What kind of a fool was I to want Clarice Bosworth's cast-off beaus? Especially *this* one, surely the most conceited, infuriating man I'd ever met. "Well, I'll thank you to stay out of my way, then. With any luck, I'll not see you until I'm on my way to Philadelphia. Never will be entirely too soon."

"Why don't you do yourself a favor and make your departure immediate, Lady Architect?"

"Who do you think you are, talking to me like that?" I fumed.

"It may be dangerous for you to stay." His voice sounded suddenly menacing to me. "For once in your life, take a man's advice . . ."

"Who are you to tell me to leave?"

"I'm not *telling* you. I'm strongly suggesting. For your own good. The house is nearly finished now. Boggs can do the rest. Why don't you . . ."

"Well, *I* strongly suggest you get out of here. Now," I screamed.

He shrugged and still smiling his superior smile, opened my lovely oval-glassed door and went out, closing it smartly behind him.

I sat down on the bottom step, shaking with anger. Had he been *warning* me? Or was he taking advantage of everything that had happened to me to try to scare me away? I would not put it past him to try to have me abandon the house so I'd lose the contest, I thought furiously. But surely that was far-fetched. Still, the attempts on my life had *happened*. The designs for the house *had* been cut into a thousand pieces. And someone had been responsible.

He was terrible! I never wanted to see him again! How could anyone be so cruelly arrogant as to kiss me like that and then laugh at me. I burst into sudden tears. He was truly awful! I hated him. But how my heart had soared when he kissed me!

I was awakened at dawn the next morning by a persistent knocking at my bedroom door. Struggling up from sleep, I drew on my robe and thrust my feet into slippers, then went to open the door.

Mary was standing there, her hair covered by a muslin nightcap, her soft brown eyes troubled.

"What is it, Mary? Is someone sick?"

"No, miss. But someone jest knock on George and my bedroom winder. We sleep back of the kitchen, you know. George, he open it up and a man say the Tyndall house is on fire. We to wake you up right away."

"What?" I pulled the tie of my robe tight and pushed past Mary toward the steps. "Have you called the fire department?"

"George is doing it now. He say to get you."

"Who was the man who came to tell us?" I cried, already halfway down the steps.

"We didn't know. We couldn't rightly see. It was still so dark and he had his hat down and his shoulders all scrunched up like he was cold. There's heavy frost this morning," she added.

I didn't wait to hear any more. I ran the rest of the way down the stairs and across the hall, quickly unlocking the front door and tearing out into the street. The sky to the north was tinged with red. My house! My beautiful, beautiful house. Pray God it wasn't too late to save it.

There was a dusting of snow on the wooden sidewalks and my thin slippers were quickly soaked. I ran frantically up the street, passing the Beaver mansion. Just as I reached the end of a long boxwood hedge that bordered

the Beaver property, someone reached out from behind
and grabbed me in powerful arms, pressing a cloth over
my mouth and nose. It was reeking with chloroform.

I struggled in vain. Indeed, my exertion only made me
breathe the stultifying cloth deeper. Gradually, my strug-
gles became more and more difficult and finally, I could
no longer fight at all. I was only dimly aware of having
the cloth being tied across my face and myself being
dragged across rough ground.

The next thing I remembered was the sudden awareness of being in icy water. A sudden, jolting, jarring,
bitter-cold wetness brought me rapidly back to consciousness.

I opened my eyes to green, smarting water and reached
up to tear the cloying gag from my face. I struggled instinctively upward and surfaced to find myself facing a
sheer rock ledge. I looked about me desperately. I was in
the quarry! At the upper end where there was no way
out. I had been a long time beating my way to the surface
and pushing the dazed confusion from my foggy brain; I
realized I'd been very deep. Probably, I'd been hurled
from the cliff above. I leaned my head back in the icy
water but if there was someone up there, he'd not waited
to see if I surfaced. There would soon be people swarm-
ing all over the area trying to put out the fire. Likely
he'd wanted to get away from the vicinity.

He was a fool, I thought scornfully. I had only to swim
out. I turned in the water and started off toward the far
end of the quarry where the lower bank offered numerous
handholds. There was certainly no way of getting out
here where I'd been thrown in. I was incredibly cold, indeed, there was a thick rime of ice all about the edge of

the quarry, and my heavy velvet robe hampered me greatly. I realized I'd have to shed it if I were to make the other end and reached to undo the heavy silken rope-like cord at the waist. It was then that the cramp hit me.

It was almost paralyzing. My legs convulsed into rigid bands so painful that I gasped and nearly went under the water again. It was too bitterly cold! I'd never last long enough to reach the far end. My assailant . . . my *murderer* had realized that. I remembered Alice telling me folks had drowned in the quarry in mid-summer because the spring-fed waters were so deep and cold. I struggled desperately back toward the cliff, gasping with pain and cold. If I could just find a handhold. Anything to grasp until help came. If it ever did, I thought despairingly, but fighting for life, I scratched at the sheer rock wall above me.

Then, almost as if in answer to my prayers, I saw a partially submerged bush. A mere arm's length of bare branch, really, the result of a seed falling into a cleft in the rock. I grasped at it with almost my last strength. My hands were so terribly, terribly cold, and supporting all my weight, they were quickly losing every bit of sensation. I'd soon lose my grasp and slip beneath the surface.

I began to scream, then, but my frantic cries echoed mockingly from the opposite cliff. First one hand and then the other, benumbed into near uselessness, slipped away from my tiny hold on life. I couldn't last! I began to cry feebly. Then my long silken robe cord floated lazily to the surface. I stared at it in desperation, then realizing I could use it to *tie* myself to the bush, I began frantically tugging at it until I freed it from my waist. Somehow, my desire to live giving me strength, I managed to knot it about my chest under my arms and lash it to the bush. It drew me against the face of the cliff, my cheek right against the cold, gray surface.

I was temporarily safe. But probably all I'd done was to prolong my misery. There would be too much excitement at the house with a fire to fight for anyone to notice I was missing. And by the time the fire was out and anyone *did*, I'd long since have died in the icy waters. Already my body was losing vital warmth and I felt drowsy, lethargic. I no longer attempted to scream. Useless anyhow. There was no one to hear me. I let my breath out on a long sob, let my head slump backward against my aching shoulders and lost awareness again.

I don't know how long I'd hung there when I awoke again, this time to find myself being worried and pulled. I was almost angry at the annoyance. I was weary. I wanted to sleep. I began to cry peevishly.

"Help me, my dear. I can't do it alone. Can you release the cord?" a dear, familiar voice was saying.

I opened my eyes and saw Mr. Bosworth's concerned eyes above me. He was trying desperately to pull me into a small rowboat. His white hair stood on end and his thin face wore an expression of anxiety. The boat was listing dangerously toward me. "You must help me, Minerva. Tear the cord free. I can't reach it," he ordered.

I reached up and fumbled at the cord. My hands felt as if they were encased in bread dough. They kept falling away uselessly. I sobbed in frustration. But at last, the little bush itself broke off from my repeated tugs at the cord and threw me back precipitantly into the boat, almost capsizing it, roots and all landing in my face.

I struggled to pull myself erect. Mr. Bosworth reached toward me to help me get the entangling bush free of my clothing, when something bobbed lazily against the side of the boat. He and I turned to look at the same time and my scream was drowned out by his. The bush at the surface of the water had evidently concealed something and when I pulled it loose, the terrible secret had surfaced at last. Slowly bobbing on the surface was a body, silent and macabre. Its long, gray hair floated lazily on the icy green water and around its neck was a blue woolen scarf, pulled brutally tight, tight enough to have killed its wearer.

CHAPTER 8

Somehow we managed to get the body of Mrs. Bosworth, for her husband's strangled cry of "Jenny" identified her, into the little rowboat.

"Thank God, the boat was here," Mr. Bosworth mumbled dazedly as we rowed painfully back. "The lads use it to fish for the catfish that live here." Then he stared down at the sodden body of his wife, almost perfectly preserved by the icy waters in spite of over a year in the quarry, and started to sob wrenchingly.

We managed somehow to beach the boat, Mrs. Bosworth's body still crumpled in the bottom of it for we were both too spent and cold to take it out. I lay on the rocky bank, teeth chattering with cold while Mr. Bosworth moved jerkily about, finding dry wood to start a fire. In a short time, he had a roaring one going and I drew near, desperately trying to get warm. Mr. Bosworth kept piling wood on, tears running slowly down his lined cheeks. When my teeth had stopped chattering so fiercely, he sat down beside me.

"What happened, Minerva?" he asked quietly. "How did you come to be in the quarry?"

I told him briefly about the mysterious visitor to his house who'd come to tell us the Tyndall house was on fire.

"I should have realized it was a decoy," I said miserably. "I ran right into his arms."

He shook his head sadly. "Thank God you were still alive when I got here," he said.

"How did you know where to look for me, sir?"

For a moment, he looked dazed. Then his eyes traveled to the silent form in the boat. "Jenny came and woke me," he said quietly. "She shook me by the shoulder and said, 'Jonathon, go help that poor girl. She's in the quarry and can't get out.'"

I felt the wet hair on the back of my neck crawl at his words. Was the poor old man mad? Yet, what other explanation was there? He must have arrived at the scene almost as quickly as I'd been thrown in; as cold as the water was, I'd have been frozen to death otherwise. I stared at him in speechless wonder.

He stood up and walked to the rowboat. He lifted the body out and laid it on the beach, doing what he could to compose it. The gentle, pretty old face was serene. She seemed to be sleeping peacefully. With a great gulping sob, Mr. Bosworth folded the little hands, then placed his own gnarled ones over them. I got up and went to his side, putting my arm about his shoulders.

"We've got to get back, Mr. Bosworth. We'll need help to get her home," I said gently.

He stared at me, his usually bright eyes dull with pain. "She's dead, Minerva. She's really dead!" he said.

I got to my feet, drawing him with me, my sodden arm about the frail old shoulders. "Yes, sir. I'm so dreadfully sorry," I said pityingly.

He seemed to struggle to gain control of himself. Then, straightening up, he put his arm across my shoulders as if to assist me. Together, we made our way back up the rough track to the path above the quarry.

"It's all right," he said reassuringly. "It's all right now."

I'm so relieved to know at last what happened. I . . . I fear I've been a bit confused for some time now. I kept thinking perhaps she'd just gotten lost . . . or was angry with me. You see, we didn't always get on so well. I kept hoping she'd come back to me." He smiled through his tears and helped me over a fallen tree. "She looked . . . just grand when she woke me, though. So pretty. So very pretty. And I could tell she was quite well and happy. Only a little agitated because you were in danger, and she wanted me to help you. I promise you, Minerva, when the time comes, I'll not be afraid to go on where she is."

It was many days before I was really well again.

When we'd finally reached the Bosworth house, everyone but Annette and Mary had gone to the fire. Annette had been forbidden by her father, and so Mary had stayed to look after her.

The little woman helped me strip off my sodden clothes and rubbed me dry before shooing me into bed with heated bricks at my feet. She turned up the gas log and left Annette and Mr. Bosworth with me while she ran up to the fire to get Jon.

He came back quickly with the welcome news that the fire was already out. It had been started in a pile of building materials in the lean-to the men had erected at the rear of the house. There was no damage to the house whatsoever.

"But you, Minerva. I fear complications may result from this," he said worriedly. "It'll be a miracle if pneumonia doesn't develop. You lost vital body heat even in that short time you were submerged."

He proved to be right. By evening, I had developed a fever and in the morning, they later told me, I was delirious and didn't know where I was. I was sick for three days before I passed the crisis and came out of my oblivion. And by that time, Mrs. Bosworth had been laid to rest and the family had settled back into a sorrowful routine.

Mr. Bosworth came to see me. I was struck by the peace in his fine old face. "It was a miracle, Minerva," he said simply. "She wanted to save you. Obviously, there must have been someone in the family better equipped than I to have rescued you, but it was *me* she came to. Because I loved her best," he said proudly.

"I'm sure of it, Mr. Bosworth," I said, patting his hand. "And I'm grateful to you both. I would have been dead very shortly."

"Well, you're going to be all right now. Although Jon says you must stay in bed for at least another week. The house is faring very well without you; it's nearly done."

I frowned and shook my head. "I'm afraid there might be another attempt to do something to it . . . or me."

"You will never be left alone in this house. And it will be thoroughly locked at night. Jon and I both have our hunting rifles loaded in our rooms. As for the other house, Bill has posted a guard at night. Although the fire wasn't really set *in* the house. It seemed that was just a ruse to lure you out to where the killer could get you."

I shuddered in spite of myself. "What about your wife, sir?" I asked quietly. "It appeared to me that her scarf had been used to . . . to . . ."

He stared down at his hand on the coverlet. "Yes. It had been drawn tightly enough to make her lose consciousness, the coroner said, but the actual cause of death was drowning. There was a fragment of rope about her ankle. He theorizes that the body was weighted and thrown into the quarry. Of course we weren't assuming foul play then, and had she simply fallen into it, her body would have floated to the surface."

"Then, the rope must have frayed against something on the bottom, and she floated up only to catch against the little bush," I finished.

"It seems that way."

He was silent, staring out the window to the trees where the maple buds showed red against the sky. "Your finding her like that was a great blessing for me, Minerva," he said at last. "I . . . I think Jenny would feel well repaid for the effort it must have been for her to 'get back' to me in your behalf. I'm sure she's happy to see that I'm quite my old self again."

I struggled upright and embraced him. There were tears in my eyes so that I couldn't see him very well. "I'm glad, too, Mr. Bosworth," I said.

Two days later I awoke before dawn with a feeling of strength and well-being. I had been in bed for nearly a week and Jon had insisted I stay for several days more. But I felt perfectly well at last.

I got out of bed quietly and padded in bare feet to the window. Opening it, I leaned out and breathed in the sweet April air. It had become warmer while I was confined to bed and the birds were singing as if determined each to outdo its fellows. It was a lovely day. And, suddenly, I wanted to see what progress had been made on the house.

I dressed quietly, thinking perhaps it was foolhardy of me to go to the site alone. But everyone knew I'd been sick; whoever had tried to kill me would certainly not expect me to be out at this hour of the morning. Moreover,

Bill Tyndall had posted a round-the-clock guard on the house. I would not be alone.

I let myself out of the silent house, walking slowly, still a bit shaky in the knees, but well aware I was on the mend. Early hyacinths and crocuses bloomed along the boxwood hedge at Governor Beaver's mansion, and I filled my lungs with the sweet, blossom-scented air. I shuddered as I passed the place I'd been seized and hurried on past, the quicker to reach the Tyndall house and the company of the guard.

The air was soft and misty, caressing the earth to life again. The house stood against the sky, the few fine old trees we'd left standing for shade accenting it. The white limestone was in place and the cedar shingles were partially up. I noticed with pleasure that the narrow leaded window I'd specified for the hall had arrived and was in place.

The guard was waiting for his replacement on the front porch, his head bent over his knees. I smiled as I recognized young Seth Matthews.

"I'm afraid an arsonist would have slipped by and finished the house while you were sleeping, Seth," I said teasingly as I stepped up onto the porch.

He scrambled to his feet in embarrassment. "Ah, I wasn't sleepin', Miss Stewart," he said shamefacedly. "Things have been as quiet as Bellefonte on a Sunday, though."

"I'm glad to hear that."

"It's good to see you up and around, Miss Stewart, but I understand they were all afraid someone was out to get you. Should you be wandering about alone like this?"

"I'm not alone now, Seth. You're here," I said, passing him and opening the door.

"Well, I won't leave until someone comes to relieve me, miss. You can rest at ease."

I thanked him and went on into the house.

I walked through the downstairs rooms, noting the progress that had been made in my absence. Thank heaven the house hadn't been set afire. But would the Tyndalls be forced to keep an armed guard on duty in order to be allowed to live in the house in peace? My eyes misted suddenly. I certainly hadn't envisioned so much trouble when I designed the house. What was behind all the mysterious things that had happened? Why had Mrs. Bosworth been murdered? What possible connection did I have with all this? And my house? The only common denominator seemed to be the Tyndalls. They alone were connected with me, the house, Mrs. Bosworth and the mine. But how did that make us all so vulnerable? Who except Tam Whitney could be behind all the malice and danger? Suddenly, I couldn't wait to leave Bellefonte. Too much had happened to me here. I'd built my first house and although it had . . . or would win me national recognition, it had brought me much pain, too. I'd suffered illness and injury because of it. And, because I'd come here to design it, I'd met Anthony Richmond. I'd fallen in love, and had my heart broken.

Well, the house would be done soon. And then there would be nothing to keep me here. I'd get on the train and go back to Philadelphia. And, I told myself resolutely, I'd not waste time in futile yearning. I had a life to live. Work to do. I choked back the sob that rose in my throat.

I climbed the stairs to the second floor, admiring the simple beauty of the pine stairs and bannisters. It was a beautiful house. The early morning sun shone through the casement windows warming the pine to molten honey. I prayed silently that whatever dark shadow hung over it would soon be lifted and that the Tyndalls would have many happy years here.

I turned to the left at the top of the stairs into the room which was to be a library-study. Beyond it to the right was a large bedroom-playroom for Annette. The master bedroom was connected by a door, again on the right. It was possible to go from one room to the other and come out again in the hall at the top of the stairs, the three rooms all having connecting doors. To the right as one stood at the top of the stairs was a fourth room and the bathroom.

The pine staircase continued on to the third floor where there were four more rooms. I started on up, pausing on the landing to gaze out at the Nittany mountain range across the valley. It was charcoal and purple in the early morning light, serene and unchanging. The view from the front of the house, while not as spectacular as from the rear, was restful and pleasant. Happy Valley, the Bellefonters called it. It hadn't proved so to me.

As I stood there quietly dreaming, I heard a footstep in the downstairs hall. Then the front door shut quietly.

"Seth," I called, leaning over the rail to look down. I could see no one, yet felt a presence on the stairs. Whoever was there was clinging close to the outside of the stairwell which was not visible from above.

"Seth," I called again, more urgently, then thinking perhaps the boy's relief had come and wouldn't answer to Seth's name, I called more loudly. "Who is there?"

There was no answer. But I heard someone moving upwards, still staying close to the outside wall so he was hidden from my vision.

I turned frantically to the casement windows and wrenched one open. Seth was strolling along far down Curtin Street. Evidently whoever was now in the house was known to him, trusted by him. I leaned far out and screamed his name at the top of my lungs, but he evidently didn't hear me because he kept on going.

I slammed the window shut and dashed down to the second-floor hall, suddenly acutely aware that I was trapped if I stayed above that floor since the auxiliary service stairs stopped there. But I was already too late. My pursuer had reached the second-floor landing where both stairs from above came out. I couldn't get past him that way. I could hear him now, poised there, waiting to see if I ran to the top of the service stairs.

I saw that I was effectively cut off from escape that way. Quickly I whirled around and dashed into the library-study, realizing the window on the west opened over the porch roof. If I could only get out onto it, I might be able to drop off unhurt and at least attempt to run down Curtin Street toward help. But, reading my intentions, my pursuer loped up the stairs and came into the library-study after me. I looked back once, a mere glimpse, and saw a man's tall figure reaching out toward me. I felt his hand seize my shoulder and I wrenched loose, painfully aware I'd not reach the window before he had me. The door to Annette's bedroom was just beside me and I darted through, slamming the door violently in his face and turning the key in the new lock. Then I dashed toward the door into the master bedroom. Maybe, just maybe, I'd reach the top of the stairs before he recovered himself. But it was a futile hope. He had whirled around as soon as the key clicked in the lock and met me at the top of the steps. As I burst through the master bedroom door into the hall, I looked up in terror to confront the triumphant face of Richard Langley!

"You!" I cried, sagging against the doorframe. "You're one of the people I never once suspected. Why?"

He only laughed and stepped toward me, keeping the stairs at his back.

I lunged forward suddenly, throwing all my weight at his midsection. He was taken by surprise and tottered backward, clutching at the round newel post to save himself from falling backward down the stairs. I had a moment's respite and darted past him toward the third floor. At the landing, I jerked the casement open frantically and began screaming for help at the top of my lungs. But he was on me instantly, pulling me back from the window and slamming it shut.

"No one will hear you anyhow," he said smugly. "I volunteered to take the watch this morning. Seth will tell his relief not to hurry; he's sure to pass him on Allegheny Street."

"Then how will you explain that I was killed while you supposedly were on guard here?"

"I'll simply say someone must have slipped in the back way and pursued you up here before I realized you were in danger. I ran to your help, but it was too late. You'd already been thrown from these high windows and your murderer gave me the slip on the service stairs and escaped into the woods. I'll be thoroughly shaken and self-accusatory."

I tore frantically at his face with my nails and managed to draw blood. He relaxed his hold for a second and I escaped and ran up the last flight to the third floor. As I reached the small bedroom at the top of the steps, he pursued me and trapped me effectively. There were two small windows here, directly above the casements on the third floor landing. That and the doorway which he now blocked were the only exits. I sank to the floor in despair, realizing that I was trapped at last.

"Good girl, Minerva. You may as well rest for a moment," he said silkily.

"I promise you, you'll have a fight on your hands before you throw me out of these windows," I said desperately. "And you're already bleeding. Don't you think your story of some unknown person killing me might not hold up?"

He put a hand up to his face and smiled. "Scratches sustained as I ran through the woods pursuing your vile murderer."

I stared at him with a growing sense of hopelessness. Who would ever suspect him? I certainly hadn't.

"Before I die, would you mind telling me why?" I asked bleakly.

"The land, my dear, the *land*," he said. "There's a wide vein of extremely rich iron ore running through these hundred acres. With the abundance of coal for smelting, it's worth a fortune. I'd been quietly conducting tests preparatory to buying the land when, out of the blue, Bill Tyndall bought it to build his house."

"Why didn't you simply tell him you had been planning to buy it? He's a gentleman and would have sold it to you."

His laugh was ugly, cynical. "You are terribly naïve. He was delighted with his purchase, and had I attempted to buy it, he'd have been tipped off that it had greater value than as real estate. I didn't dare tell him about the iron ore. I tried to stir up ill feeling against him in discreet ways at the mine, thinking if he was disliked, he'd leave Bellefonte. The men already hated Roberts; it was easy to transfer their dislike to a newcomer. Then there was the mysterious and sudden death . . ."

"Did you have anything to do with that?" I asked fearfully.

"Of course. He'd seen me talking to Mrs. Bosworth the day she disappeared. I had been unaware of it, you see. He'd been walking his dog. Later, he began to wonder why I didn't mention having seen her. He confronted me with it one day when we were working alone in the mine office. I had to kill him. Then I took his body to the mine and threw him down a shaft."

"Then you *did* kill Mrs. Bosworth, too?" I said, feeling sick. "But why her? A gentle old lady?"

He shrugged his shoulders. "She came upon me digging samples out of the ground on the land her son-in-law had just bought. I had the paraphernalia to make tests. You know, test tubes and such. She was an iron-master's daughter herself and realized exactly what I was doing. I couldn't let her tell what she'd seen. There'd have been no chance of my getting the land then." He frowned suddenly. "I weighted her body. It was ill luck that it broke free and rose to the surface."

"To trap her killer," I said steadily.

He laughed unpleasantly. "Never. You'll die, too, and, no doubt, my nice convenient scapegoat, Tam Whitney, will be blamed."

"How will my death profit you?" I said. "I don't understand why *I* was your target."

"I'd hoped to convince Bill he wasn't wanted in Bellefonte. But he won the miners' confidence. All but poor, deranged Whitney. When that didn't work, I thought I could frighten you away. A timid woman, after all, would naturally be terrified when threatened . . . her work destroyed. But you, too, were pluckier than I'd expected, so the only answer seemed to be your tragic death."

"Why? That wouldn't change anything."

"You don't know the Tyndalls very well if you think that. They'd never live in this house if they thought you'd died in the building of it. The minute you were gone, they'd have put it on the market. As their good friend and well-wisher, I'd have taken it off their hands, and then later, after a long enough interval not to arouse suspicion, I'd have stumbled upon the discovery of the iron ore."

"I think all this is too fantastic. You haven't reasoned like a normal person," I said a little wildly. "You seem to have gone out of your way to be deceitful, destructive. It could all have been so simple. If you'd only told Bill of your discovery. I'm sure he'd have gone partners with you . . ."

"You are hopelessly trusting," he said harshly. "It hasn't been my experience in life that anyone's likely to treat you fairly."

"Bill Tyndall has treated you fairly," I said spiritedly. "It was he who recommended you for your last promotion. Alice told me so."

"That money came from Roberts' pocket, not his. And, why should I share with him what is rightfully mine anyway?"

He moved menacingly toward me. "Anyhow, enough of this. It's foolish for you to want to know all my motives. You are in your last moments anyhow."

I hitched myself backward from him warily. He lunged downward toward me and pulled me erect, bruising my arms as he forced me toward the windows. I whirled toward him, again raking at his face with my fingernails. I would not die easily, I promised myself. But he overpowered me, grabbed both my wrists in his and forced me backward, inexorably backward toward the windows, fifty feet above the ground. I closed my eyes, knowing I would die now, unbelieving, yet praying for acceptance, trying to unite myself with God at this hour of my death. I stiffened my back, praying, crying, fighting, but being forced back until I felt the cold panes against my back.

It was then that the shot rang out.

His hands dropped away and he slumped to the floor, leaving me nearly supine against the low windows. I looked up over his fallen body toward the doorway. Anthony Richmond stood there, smoking revolver in hand.

He dropped the gun and ran across the room, stepping over the inert form to lift me in his arms.

"Are you all right, Minerva?" he cried anxiously.

"I'm quite all right," I sobbed, burying my face against his shoulder.

He lifted me across Richard Langley's body and carried me out of the room, down my steps in the tower and into the front hall. Only then did he release me and deposit me on the bottom step, sitting down beside me, his arm around my shoulders. Then he turned me and encircled me so that I lay tenderly against his chest. His eyes stared down anxiously into mine. I noticed his jaw contracting. There was gentleness in his dark eyes and concern.

"Thank God I was in time," he said.

"Lucky for me you were nearby," I sobbed nervously.

"Not luck, Minerva. Planning. Watching. Day and night. I'm sorry I didn't come in and stop him immediately. Like a fool, I didn't realize you had anything to fear from him until you screamed. Then I had to move carefully because he had you. I was afraid he'd hurt you . . ."

"You've been watching me?" I said in bewilderment.

"Ever since Mr. Bosworth pulled you from the quarry. Up until then, I thought someone was just trying to chase you away out of malice they bore Bill. Like you, I assumed it was Tam Whitney. But once you were thrown into the quarry with no hope of getting out, I knew someone was trying to kill you."

"But you never even came near me. All the time I was sick," I mourned childishly.

"*You* told me you never wanted to see me again," he reminded me, a trace of his old teasing in his eyes.

"I lied," I said, not caring that I was giving him ammunition to use against me.

He laughed delightedly. "I'm so glad you're safe now," he said, cradling me close. "God, it's been awful, not knowing who was after you or why."

"He wanted the land. He found iron ore here. He killed Mrs. Bosworth, too . . ." I began.

He kissed my eyelids gently. "I know. I heard a good bit of it while I was creeping up on him. Don't think about it now. It's over, thank God."

He kissed me then and it wasn't like the first time. I was too emotionally exhausted. But it was very good. I knew that he was neither laughing at me nor despising me. I lay spent in his arms, letting my own deep happiness wash over me.

"I love you, Minerva," he said humbly. "And I beg your pardon for ever hurting you. You were quite right in everything you said to me. Men who demand a woman's adulation should be willing to return it in kind. I *did* laugh at you because your being good at your job seemed to diminish me. It's hard to admit, Minerva, and I know I have a long way to go before I truly stand on my own merits. But will you let me try? Will you give me a chance to prove my love and devotion? Without, I promise you, ever trying to put you down again."

For answer, I burst into tears. I'd longed to see the

haughty Anthony humbled, gleefully dreamed of taking sweet revenge on him for all the humiliation he'd caused me, yet now all I could do was bask in the wondrous sweetness of his declaration of love.

"Minerva, darling, I don't blame you for crying," he said unhappily. "What right do I have to think you'd want to marry a cad like me? But will you at least consent to stay in Bellefonte and become my business partner? Perhaps, in time, I can convince you I'm reformed. Perhaps I might even be able to win your love."

"Oh, Anthony, you already *have* that," I wailed. "And why did you ask me to be your partner? Is it because my design won an award, and you know I'll be good for business?"

"Yes," he said quite frankly. "I *knew* your work was good, but my own bigotry made me prejudiced and blind about it. When you won the award out of all the entries in this great country, I was forced to look at your work objectively. And to admit it was very good."

"But you called this house fantastic."

"The adjective was all wrong, darling. It is like you. Wonderful. Unique. Useful. Original. Lovely." With each word, he dropped a kiss on my eyelids, cheeks, throat.

It was hard to be practical at such a time, but I struggled valiantly to think like a true business woman. "If . . . if I accept your offer of a business partnership, will it jeopardize the earlier offer of marriage?" I asked breathlessly.

He was murmuring against my ear. "Of course not, darling. We'll simply install a cradle in the main office," he said.

Millie J. Ragosta and her family (her husband and seven of their eleven children) moved to Bellefonte, Pennsylvania, a few years ago. There they purchased an old house (on Curtin Street), and it was here that Millie, while researching the history of the home, was inspired to write this novel. The house on Curtin Street was, in fact, designed by a woman architect named Minerva Parker and the story behind it lends itself wonderfully to a suspenseful novel. Millie J. Ragosta, in addition to an active family life, is author of several books and a dedicated collector of antiques, restoring many of them herself.